BEARERS OF BAD TIDINGS

Also by Martin Hart

Rats

BEARERS OF BAD TIDINGS

A story of father and son

by

MARTIN HART
Translated by J.W. Arriens

ALLISON & BUSBY
LONDON · NEW YORK

First published in Great Britain 1983 by
Allison & Busby Ltd
6a Noel Street
London W1V 3RB
and distributed in the USA
by Schocken Books Inc
200 Madison Avenue, New York, NY 10016

Copyright ©1979/1984 by Maarten 't Hart and B.V.
Uitgeverij De Arbeiderspers, Amsterdam.
Translation copyright ©1984 J.W. Arriens and Allison &
Busby Ltd

British Library Cataloguing in Publications Data
    Hart, Martin
    Bearings of bad tidings
    I. Title II. De aansprekers. *English*
    839.3'1364 F   PT5881.18.A/

ISBN 0-85031-534-4

Set in 10/11½pt Plantin by Top Type Phototypesetting Co. Ltd,
London W1.
Printed in Great Britain by Billings & Son Limited,
Worcester.

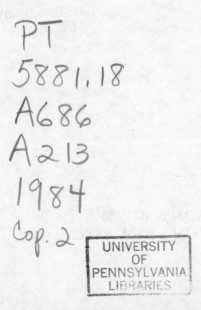

Contents

The Dutch title of this autobiographical novel is *De Aansprekers*. *Aansprekers*, or *aanzeggers* as they are also called, were undertakers' men who used to go from door to door, especially in the villages, officially informing relatives and friends of a bereavement on behalf of the family. For this purpose they wore a top hat and black suit, and they must have been a familiar and impressive sight. Now the custom has all but died out.

There is no English equivalent of the term. The title in Dutch is a play on words, referring to the two principal characters in the story: the father, by profession a municipal gravedigger, and therefore loosely an *aanspreker*, and his son, who learns of his father's terminal cancer and must decide whether or not to convey the bad tidings to him.

Sometimes while walking in the streets alone you look towards the sky and silent roofs and feel you could quite easily touch the clouds: an instant when existence is so real that it appears no time will ever come of stillness greater even than in sleep. But birds swoop down to settle on the roofs and round the corner comes an old, old man.

1
The quayside

During the festive season in December, I suddenly began to dream of ships that slipped noiselessly from the quay before I could go on board. When I woke up I knew something was wrong, but I could not tell what. Every evening shortly before eight I would become uneasy and the ships would drive me into the streets, where I would wander aimlessly for an hour or so. But my wanderings failed to reveal what was preoccupying me or what was wrong. I had the absurd notion that I would only get to the bottom of it if I were to walk along a quayside, with the smell of flour and tar oil in my nostrils. The day after New Year's Day I visited my mother to wish her a happy new year. I arrived in late afternoon and stayed to eat, and was startled by my acute sense of happiness. Nothing had changed, which made me happy; the clock ticked away just as impressively as before, and the door might at any moment open to admit my father. If he entered I would say: "Whereas we live in these circumstances...."

He had never finished the sentence and I had never asked how it finished, not because I wasn't curious, but because I felt I could guess: whereas we live in these circumstances we should resign ourselves to the inevitable. He had used the word live; and try as I might I could not accept that he was dead.

"I'll just slip outside again," I said after the meal.

"In this weather?" my mother asked.

"It's dry," I said.

"Yes, but it's bitterly cold."

But she was already holding open the door for me and waved as I left, even though I would be returning the same evening; and I walked through the streets all alone, that Sunday evening. Many people still appeared to be celebrating the day after New Year's Day, for in all sorts of houses I saw groups of people sitting around festive tables on

9

which the candlelight was reflected in the table-silver. After passing just three such houses I could feel my spirits lifting. If I were to pass 365 houses in which people were celebrating, there was a chance that I might be spared dreams of ships leaving without me for an entire year — at least if above the houses I saw the spire of the Great Church. The church clock chimed with calm strokes as I was walking along the dyke, and it was as though I could smell each individual stroke. Perhaps that was because at each stroke I inhaled deeply. The smell of flour and tar oil was already on the air; in a moment, on the quayside, I would almost be able to feel it.

On one of the houses on the dyke there were lights strung around the window-frame; through the lights I could see into a room where a boy and a girl were standing alone, although the table was laid for a number of people. The girl was wearing an ankle-length red dress. She stood at arm's length from the boy, with her hands resting on his shoulders; their eyes followed the same path and they looked only at each other, each so enraptured it almost made me sad. Her red dress made her look taller than he was, even though he towered over her.

"As though she had descended from heaven," I muttered as I passed on, and shivers ran down my back because I could still see those fond, warm glances in front of me.

"They should stay like that for ever," I said quietly. "Then they might just have a chance of remaining happy." Did I say that because I was walking past Thijs Loosje's house? Surely that had not even crossed my mind: I only thought of it as I was passing his house and he appeared in the doorway, recognizing me straight away.

"Congratulate me!" he said. "It's fifty years ago today that I slipped the ring on to her finger. I'm off to see her. A big celebration tonight, you understand — just us two."

I shook his hand and asked, "Why just you two? Won't there be any relatives?"

"All dead, we're the only ones left because...."

"Yes, yes," I said, interrupting him, "I understand," because I did not want to hear what he had been about to say, and I walked on as he locked his front door.

I walked more briskly. All day there had been a threatening sky and, curiously enough, it began to rain softly just as I reached the harbour. But I walked on steadily, unaware of any danger. I made my way towards the middle of the quayside which, because the water occasionally crept up the quay at high tide, had been built on a slight

10

slope so that the water automatically ran back if the moon produced flood-tides.

It was high-tide now, I saw, but the water would not rise far today. There was still at least a metre and a half between the quay and the water-level. I walked on unconcernedly, even though I realized the going was getting trickier because the rain was beginning to freeze on the stones. I was forced to walk more and more slowly so as not to lose my footing. This did not bother me for there was not a soul to be seen. The quayside was mine and would remain mine alone now that black ice had begun to form. Nobody would dare venture outdoors any more. The thought suddenly made me feel so happy that I broke into a little skip in the middle of the quay. In that one, fleeting moment in which I left the ground I knew the gesture to have been a mistake, and I prepared myself for a heavy fall. All my limbs were braced: I raised my arms but I did not fall over when I landed, my body instead going into such odd gyrations that for a second or two I lost all sense of where my limbs and head were normally located. Once I was fairly sure again where my head was, I observed that I was still upright and that I was gliding over the quay towards the water. It was a most pleasant sensation, especially because it was happening so slowly. By now it was as smooth as glass. I lifted one foot up to take a step, but that only made me lurch again and I threatened to fall over.

"Well, I'll be damned," I muttered. I was still sliding towards the water and realized I would have to do something soon or ridiculous though it might seem I would end up in the cold, stinking waters of the Meuse. Once again I attempted to take a step, lifting my right foot off the ground as little as possible, but I instantly realized it was out of the question. I tried to struggle clear by shuffling along, and managed to make some headway, but in doing so only succeeded in sliding more rapidly towards the edge of the quay. At that moment, I felt the first sense of panic; I realized that I was simply doomed to slide into the water and that there was nothing I could do about it. But I instantly rejected the idea. It was too absurd: I was in the middle of the quayside and might be sliding down slowly, but surely it was not beyond me to escape from the grip of that glassy pavement.

While the thought was going through my mind I suddenly heard the sound of a falling body. Across the water I could see a dark figure lying on the road. He — or was it a she? I could not tell — tried to get up but fell down again. There was something droll about the figure's movements, something that invited laughter, but I was unable to

11

laugh and was instead envious because that person was lying in a spot where the quayside did not slope as it did here. Nevertheless the figure, which was still trying vainly to stand up, gave me an idea. If I too were to fall over, or, more accurately, were to sit down on the cobblestones, would I then not be able to stop sliding? I might even be able to crawl on hands and knees to the footpath in front of the houses, where I would be safer. I could always grab a window-ledge, or might even be able to walk. But it soon became apparent that I could not even flop down on to the pavement, and I saw as well that any movement I made only resulted in my slipping more rapidly towards the water. Even so, I was still not really worried, partly because, as long as I did not move, I was sliding so slowly that it was scarcely perceptible. I seemed to be taking at least a minute over each cobblestone, and there were still so many cobblestones between me and the edge of the quay that I felt as though I had aeons of time. Enough time, at least, to think of ways of getting out of this rather desperate situation.

"Oh, of course not really desperate," I said in an undertone, but I quickly swallowed the last words because even speaking accelerated the sliding. Somebody was sure to come to my aid before I ended up in the water, or somebody would glance out of one of those illuminated windows — plenty of houses here, and lots and lots of windows. People were celebrating behind those windows and all at once I could no longer feel glad I was not taking part. I felt anything was better than sliding impotently like this — even a dinner with lots of people and laughter and talking, even speeches. But why should I get worked up: before I reached the water there was sure to be an irregularity in the pavement or there would be a rough cobblestone on which I could arrest my slide. And even if I were to fall into the water: so what? I could swim. I looked at the water; patches of oil winked at me. I felt uneasy. It might be high tide, but I would not be able to get back out of the water on to the quay at all easily; the gap between the water-level and the quay was too great. And even if I did, I would once again be confronted with the glassy quay. I would, of course, be able to swim to the other side, but there the quay was at least a metre higher and I would not be able to get up at all.

Once again I had a feeling of panic, and I shivered suddenly. The only thing that kept me from falling was the fact that I was sliding so very slowly, and the sense of panic gave way to a strange, almost blissful clarity of thought which, I knew only too well, could at any moment revert to the blackest despair. But this was too absurd: it couldn't be happening — and anyway, I had never heard of anything like it before. Young man slides down quayside and drowns in icy water. If I were in a car it would be a different matter, but this was too much: it would be downright unfair. I was just a pedestrian who had wanted to stretch his legs, a worrier who had gone for a stroll to try and stop brooding. I had now slipped three cobblestones closer to the water; the church clock across the water seemed to be moving faster than I was. The dark figure was still trying to get up and much further along, level with the harbour-bridge, there was another figure on the pavement. Was he crawling? Or was he just lying there? He was so far away and it was so dark that I could not tell. In any case my attention was diverted by a bright light that suddenly appeared in a window not so very far from where I was standing. I thought I could see a figure standing behind the window, looking intently in my direction. Now I could expect help soon. What if I were to call out for help? I opened my mouth and took a deep breath but abruptly felt myself sliding so much faster that I closed my mouth as carefully as possible. Besides, I had no desire whatever to call for help, since that would have made it seem something really was wrong. I just kept on sliding, and so slowly that it would take hours — well, at least minutes — before I disappeared into the water. And even then there would still be hope. But how could there be nobody, nobody at all, to come to my aid? I had the whole quayside to myself, I reflected bitterly. It was time something happened, for I was getting cold. Above all my head was so cold that it hurt, because of the super-cooled rain which had settled in my thick hair. And my teeth had been chattering for some time, too.

Once again my feeling of clear-headedness narrowed to a sense of desperation. And once more I was able to allay the panic with a torrent of thoughts, of which memories formed a steadily greater part. All that was left was for my whole life to flit past like a film. But of course it would not come to that. Once again I looked across the quayside; once again I saw those beckoning patches of oil, which glinted with such strange beauty in the pale light shed by the streetlamps; once again I looked at the figures on the other side who were both, by now, walking and moving towards one another with infinite slowness: so slowly that one might easily have mistaken them for the mooring posts which rose up out of the water at regular intervals along the quay-wall on both sides. Mooring-posts! That was it. Why hadn't I thought of that before? For if I took extreme care I could shuffle forwards and I did so at once, even before my thoughts had reached the stage that one might term a solution. I deliberately let myself slide more quickly so as to get close to the nearest mooring-post. I shuffled forwards so quickly that I caught up with the hands of the clock, which suddenly disappeared from vision because my legs had gone from under me and my hands struck the pavement extremely painfully. I fell and began sliding rather rapidly towards the water, but was able to brake my descent a little and even to change course slightly so that eventually I made an exact landing at a mooring-post. My feet came to rest against the post, my bottom adorned the brick edge of the quay, and my hands were still behind me. I did not dare bring them round to the front, for I suspected they were bleeding. Instead I lifted them up a little and there I sat, shivering violently with my teeth still chattering. Yes; I was undoubtedly a little better off, but I felt as though there was nothing for it but to cry. All the same, I managed not to: I just felt some painful prickling in the corners of my eyes, swallowed and pulled myself together. I sat up straight. The soles of my feet were pressed firmly against the mooring-post and I felt I would never move them again.

What could I do next? I had no idea. I could not stand up — that was certain. I would have to remain sitting like that, even though I would develop cramp in my calves and my bottom would be frozen to the quay. Melted water crept into my trousers and rose higher as it became warmed. My teeth were chattering so loudly that I could not understand why the two people on the other side were not looking at me. The church clock struck once, for half-past seven, and in the gaping void on the opposite side — a street — a car approached, gliding over the road almost noiselessly and with inexorable slowness. I was caught directly in the headlights, but was able to conceal myself behind the mooring-post so that the shafts of light passed by me on either side. Somebody, I saw, was walking on the bridge, and he was walking as though nothing was the matter.

Was I afraid, or would I be able to ward off my fear by anticipating it? At any event I suddenly realized I was furious with myself. Why had I fallen for such a ridiculously mystical notion as believing that I might find a solution to my problems here on the quayside? It had nearly resulted in my getting a thorough drenching in ice-cold water. Would I never be any wiser? There had been no reason whatever for my going on an outing to this mirror-smooth quayside, but meanwhile here I was shivering at the waterside with no idea what to do next. It might even have been possible to stand up and walk away but I no longer dared try. Only now did it become apparent how deeply terrified I had been at sliding so impotently. I had been quite powerless and but for the mooring-post I should now have been lying among those smirking patches of oil. All of a sudden I had a feeling that everything was somehow connected: the ships, the powerlessness and the mooring-post; yes, in a moment I would wake up. I did not have enough blankets, which was why I was shivering like that. Well, as long as I kept on trembling there was nothing to worry about. When you shiver the body produces heat in order to keep the body temperature at the right level. When you stop shivering the body ceases to feel cold, you lapse into a slumber and your temperature drops until you are dead.

What if I really were to die like that one day? It made me think of a nurse I had met not long before. She told me that people about to die were often disillusioned and said: was that really all it was, was that life? At the time I thought, though vaguely, that you should only do things of which you could say at the moment of dying: that was really worthwhile. One could not live along those lines and yet it turned out not to have been an empty idea. No: I might not have been in mortal terror but I had received a great shock, which had made me tick off the things in my life that had been worthwhile. How strange; so much had happened — all the beautiful music I had heard, all the books I had read — but it all meant nothing compared with the one thing that seemed really to matter, and which was made up of white clouds drifting past high above me in a hard blue sky and the sun low over the river and the sound of moving bicycle tyres and the voice of my father behind me because I was sitting on a board he had mounted specially for me between the handlebars of his bicycle. What should have made it so special, setting it apart from everything else, I do not know; perhaps it was the motion, perhaps it was the fragrance of a summer evening, perhaps it was the blissful feeling of total security because behind me my father was protecting me with his enormous body, perhaps on account of the illusion of being able to help steer because I was allowed to hold the handlebars: but certainly one thing was his voice, singing lustily: "Daddy dear, daddy dear, won't you come home?"

Just suppose that heaven existed ... when I got there I would ask: God, may I sit in front on my father's bicycle again and ride over the dyke for ever more? Now what if my father wanted to do something totally different in heaven? But no, how could he; surely he too felt that had been the most important thing in his life and mine? It could never be re-enacted now, or if it could, only in a form in which the positions were reversed: not me in front but my son on the handlebars with me behind. It almost seemed as if I could suddenly identify those ships sailing away; but no, it could not be that, for the dyke was flanked by high flat-buildings, so that it was no longer possible to see the sun low over the river from there; and if it could not be reproduced in exactly the same form it was no use. In any case, why should I long for a son? Why should I expose somebody to life, something to which one was impotently subjected, something unsought but which nevertheless befell one. "One evening thou art there, for a woman let thee slip from her tired womb." But certain things one could resist — not the end, for that was always the same: "And one evening thou art no longer there" — but at least everything in between. It was a matter of trying to keep or take fate in your own hands and of continually avoiding being pushed about, manipulated and steered. Perhaps the illusion of being able to steer oneself was enough.

I was still shivering, but was no longer greatly troubled by the cold. I could, however, feel how tense my muscles still were and how dry my throat was. Later, in bed, I would come to realize how terrified I had been, but that was something for later: the first thing was to try and reach that bed. I ran my hand over the quay. Still like glass. Not a soul had passed by all that time, evidence enough, if I had needed any, that the quayside was completely unnegotiable. Yet I felt I did need such evidence, or I should have held myself to be a coward, a spineless creature too afraid to take any risks. Well, at least the car on the other side had stopped too, in the middle of the quay. The headlights had been switched off and in the car there were people waiting for the weather conditions to improve. Suddenly I remembered that my father had once slid into the water from this very quay in a council gritting-lorry sent out to put sand on the icy roads. He — to whom nothing ever happened — had of course managed to jump clear, but the lorry-driver had drowned.

I leaned forward. I looked into the water as though I expected still to see the gritting-lorry. But all I saw were the inevitable oil patches, which by now I hated, however beautiful they might be. How richly coloured and brilliant those fluently moving patches were! They were a little lower now, for the water was falling. Yes, it was much lower now, and I craned forward to see better. The level could not have gone down that much in half an hour: it must always have been that low, but

I could see it better now because I was closer up. There was something important to be seen, but what? Not the patches; not that mooring-post which rose so murkily out of the water, not the shiny wet quay-wall, not the ship moored much further along. But what was it then? If only I could get closer! But that was impossible. Now that the water had fallen, cross-beams had been revealed between the mooring-posts. I could, just as I had done as a child, let myself down till I was standing on the cross-beam. I did so, not because I wanted to repeat the game from my childhood of walking along the cross-beam because it was so narrow, but because I wanted to find out what there was to be seen and what it was that my brain was refusing to register. Once I was on the cross-beam I realized, with a sudden feeling of intense happiness that I had firm ground underfoot again, since black ice did not form readily on those rough beams, apart from which they were covered with a thin layer of salt that must have come from the Meuse water.

Standing up was an intense pleasure. Why had I never realized before that standing — simply standing — could be so pleasant? But what it was that was so important I still could not make out. I stood on a beam and I could even take a step, I could take two steps — heavens, what a sensation — I could move along again, and I did so, walking along the beam as I used to before, holding on to the ice-cold edge of the quay. Now and then my hands would slip but it was of no real consequence since I could lean against the quay. I walked carefully along the beam until I reached the next mooring-post, where I rested for a while. I looked at the water, turning my head around, since I had stayed facing the quay-wall while walking along. What could it be that I had seen but had been unable to comprehend? But here too I only saw those hateful oil patches. I did not know what it was I had seen a moment ago, and I could no longer see it. I picked my way along the cross-beam to the next mooring-post. Just as I was reaching it the lights of the car on the other side were switched on again. I had the feeling that they were trained on me, but of course that was not so because the car was stationary.

A man emerged from the car, who unmistakably looked towards me. He said nothing but just stood there behind the open door of the car as if to protect himself. I rested again behind the mooring-post, where I was also out of the headlights to some extent. I walked on, less cautiously now, because I did not want to be in the light of the headlights, and I would be out of their range at the next mooring-post.

Once there I did not rest but walked on as quickly as I could, driven along by the fixed beams from the headlights and the motionless figure. On I went until I reached the point near the bridge where the quay rose up and no longer sloped down towards the water. I hoisted myself up, with a mooring-post behind me in case I should slip back. It was still smooth, I noticed; very, very smooth. But that no longer mattered, for here I could sit down quietly and let myself slide because then I would only be sliding away from the quayside. Before letting myself go I looked round, at the water, and at the same instant I knew what it was I had just seen: that cross-beam. I realized that, without knowing what I did and why I was doing it, I had lowered myself on to the cross-beam and had walked along it to this point, unintentionally and without planning. I was so astounded that I forgot to push myself off and I slid towards the houses more slowly than I had meant to. Despite all my efforts to fight it back, my former feeling of terror returned at being so powerless, so much at the mercy of this marble-smooth surface, which while it served as an ice-rink leading in the right direction left me no freedom to reduce my speed or to go faster even though I tried to push myself along on the cobblestones. My hands, too, simply slid away. But it did not really matter. I reached the houses and was indeed able to get to my feet by holding on to a window-ledge. For a moment I stood still, pressed up hard against a house. I felt like embracing it, if that had been possible. Then I shuffled slowly towards the corner while those same calm strokes sounded again. Just beyond the corner I looked up. The streetlamps were illuminated but they did not seem to be casting any light. Even so I could see something that nearly took my breath away.

As far as the eye could reach, there was motionlessness: people standing in the middle of the street or on pavements and not moving. Cars too had stopped in the street, their lights on but otherwise without any sign of life. Everything seemed to have become petrified, as though at one indissoluble moment time had come to a stop. And yet there was still a vestige of movement, on a level with the streetlamps. Past the lights raindrops were falling silently, flashing briefly before disappearing into the night again: an inaudible procession of drops which lent me strength to keep shuffling and to hold out against that total immobility and eerie stillness. I shuffled along, the sole person still daring to move, unconcerned about falling.

18

2

Visiting hour

It never occurred to me that I might have drawn the curtains carelessly. I just lay there gazing contentedly and drowsily at the movements of the odd patches of sunlight on the ceiling. If I almost closed my eyes the patches changed into the glistening waterdrops you see when the first rays of the morning sun alight on dew-covered cobwebs. And if I closed my eyes altogether it was as though I could hear water murmuring. When I opened my eyes again I no longer saw the patches of sunlight on the ceiling but a moving, vertical streak of light on the wall. Was there a gap in the curtains? Or were they torn somewhere, so that the sun was shining on to the wall through the split? I might be able to find out if I were to move the curtains but then I would have to reach across the mole-hill of blankets and she might wake up. It would be better to leave that peaceful curly hair — the only thing sticking out of the blankets — undisturbed. As usual I was surprised she did not suffocate under the pile of blankets and that that was the only way she could sleep. I was also surprised at how quickly she had gone to sleep. That was how it always was; I was wide awake while she dozed off — against all the rules. And equally against the rules was the fact that I always felt so happy. None of the sadness to which Aristotle refers and which is said to be true of all animals, except the hen. Oh, no: for at least twenty minutes it was as though the past and the future fell away, and all at once you had completely fresh senses with which to listen to a song-thrush calling from far away in the woods, always repeating itself four times over, and watch the patches of light moving gently on the ceiling because the curtain was moving in the breeze. The jostling of those patches of light, I thought, that is what is meant by the "*tinzen' licht gedjoe!*" in Obe Postma's Frisian poem.

For a moment I forgot to listen to that solitary, large song-thrush and to the even more distant whirring of a cockchafer, and it was then that I heard the sound of footsteps, and it dawned on me that I had been hearing that sound all along. Soft, shuffling footsteps that did not wish to be heard. They were muffled by the lush, young grass and the pine-needles, and crept round our house until they could be heard in the yard behind the byre, and I felt how my heart, which had just calmed down, began thumping again and how I breathed in deeply. Who could be pottering around the cottage at this hour, in the middle of the day? Why should I be frightened? The cottage might not be locked but surely it was inconceivable that here in broad daylight, in the midst of the Charitable Society's woods seven kilometres from Vledder, anyone could feel the urge to overrun a small farm converted into a weekend cottage? I reached across the molehill, pulled the curtain back slightly, sat up straight and looked out of the window. In the sunny kitchen garden I saw the watchful eyes of a policeman, which might very well have been peering through the gap in the curtains for quite some time. The policeman had his cap in his hand and from the way he stood seemed not only to be looking but listening as well. He saw me; indeed, he must have seen me all that time, and I reddened. I let the curtain fall back into position and at the same moment the molehill moved.

I said, alarmed and surprised: "Police."

"Go and ask them what they want," she said matter-of-factly, and I shot out of bed, slipped into my trousers and ran in stockinged feet to the door.

When I opened the door there was another policeman there, who smiled at me in a friendly way and said: "Good afternoon, sir. I believe I've disturbed your afternoon nap?"

"I'd just woken up."

"Jolly good! May we ask you some questions?"

The other policeman came up, scratched behind his ear and put on his cap, and those two gestures instantly put me at ease. Their embarrassment was at least as great as mine.

"Yes, well, you see ..." said the first policeman and looked helplessly at his colleague.

"Sir," said the other, "we hardly need ask you really, because otherwise we would have spotted it long ago, but it's a formality; for form's sake we'd better check up a little further."

"But we already know the answer," the other said, "unless there is somebody else staying with you who has gone out."

"Somebody else here? No." My face was flushed and I was acutely conscious that the policeman kept looking at my bright red cheeks.

"There are just the two of you here?"

"Yes," I said.

"Been here for long?"

"Since Sunday."

"So there's nobody else staying with you? Oh, good afternoon, madam. I hope we are not disturbing you too much but could we have a look inside for a moment?"

"Why?" Hanneke asked.

"Madam, it's just a formality — we really know already — but it would help if we could state in our report: an inspection of the dwelling also revealed no trace of the guilty party."

He uttered the word guilty so solemnly that I instantly felt oppressed. One is, after all, always guilty — to live is to be guilty.

"What's the matter?" Hanneke asked calmly.

"Madam, I'll let you know just as soon as we've had a look inside — it's perfectly clear you've got nothing to do with it, but it would help us if we could convey that to the superintendent in black and white."

"In that case you'd better come in."

They followed us into the small farmhouse. The taller of the two policemen — the peering one — banged his head in a doorway and lost his cap, which he picked up but did not put on again. They walked calmly through the house and looked carefully at the floor in the two rooms facing the road. They inspected the hall and the kitchen and stamped on the floor of the byre so hard they they drove the redstart brooding under the beams out of its nest. That was apparently all they wanted to see and they said: "Thank you very much, we'll be on our way."

"What's up?" Hanneke asked doggedly.

"Madam, it's like this: three sheep and ten lambs have been mauled to death by an Alsatian in a field not far away, and it's our job to trace the dog. It's sure to belong to a holiday-maker, but there's no dog here, and there hasn't been one, that's pretty obvious. Please excuse the disturbance but we had no choice — the strangest things sometimes happen in these woods."

Those last words, in particular, made me doubt their story about the dog. Why did they insist so determinedly on inspecting the house if they were just looking for an Alsatian? They could have told just from walking round the house that we did not have a dog; any self-respecting dog would have raised the alarm.

"I'm afraid of dogs," I said. "I have never had a dog, and will never get one."

I saw the suspicion flare up instantly in the tall policeman's eyes. But the other one just laughed and they suddenly walked off to their blue Volkswagen, which was parked up the sandy road. We went back into the house and I quickly put on my shoes, for nothing had bothered me as much during that conversation as the fact that I was in my socks. I sat down and Hanneke said: "I'd better make some tea."

"They weren't after a dog at all."

"Of course they weren't."

"But what then?"

"What's it to us?"

That such a trivial incident should be able to throw one out so! After drinking our tea we walked through the woods. Every now and then we would see the stumpy white tails of wild rabbits light up in the undergrowth and heard the drumming of a green woodpecker. In the little fen lying quietly along the cycle track we discovered butterfly orchids in bud and sun-dew already in bloom, but I could not shake off the thought that the two policemen had had something quite different in mind. What had they been after? Did it have anything to do with what they had seen through the slightly parted curtains? But surely taking a nap in the afternoon was not an offence?

As we returned to the house we saw a cloud of dust disappearing on the sandy road. Ahead of the cloud of dust there was the grumble of a Volkswagen engine. Night was already falling: the air was crisp and fresh, the blackbird was singing its evening song, and carefree little fleecy clouds caught the last glow of the sun around the edges. Lights were on in the farm further along, which made the sandy path suddenly seem darker. The drone of the Volkswagen remained audible for a long time; so they had been back. Why?

In the house the telephone was ringing. Sometimes you can almost tell from the way a phone is ringing who is at the other end. I though: *It's my mother*, and at the same time I thought: *It cannot be my mother, because she doesn't know the number*. But it was, and her voice was subdued and dejected.

"Martin, your father's been admitted to hospital. He's to be operated on the day after tomorrow. You can still visit him tomorrow — you will come, won't you? It'll be quite a serious operation, and he would love to see you beforehand."

"Well, but he's not going to die, is he?"

"No, but still ... you can never tell."

"All right, I'll come. It will mean cycling to Steenwijk tomorrow morning and catching a train from there. But what's up, so suddenly?"

"His stomach — he has to have an operation."

And with these words whole vistas opened up before me. I saw visions of white lips — Rennies — and black lips — licorice — and thousands of mugs of warm milk that were faithfully put before my father at set times of the day, all because of his stomach which, for as long as I could remember, played up in autumn and spring. But this time he had been in pain throughout the winter as well and now, at last, after thirty years of stomach ache, he was in hospital.

All the same it was not unpleasant to have such a good pretext for leaving the house after the visit of the policemen, even though leaving might appear suspicious. We left that very evening because Hanneke's father was prepared to pick us up at Assen. We were able to stay overnight with my in-laws; the next day I took the train to Maassluis, and in the evening I drove with my mother, my sister and my brother-in-law to the hospital.

What a peaceful spring evening! Blackbirds were singing on every aerial; and there was that wonderful melancholy feeling in the air — is it a scent, or the play of the light? — that steals into one's consciousness as a presentiment of something indefinable to come, a promise of some longing. Standing in the vast entrance hall of the hospital I could still sense that scent, if it was a scent, in my nostrils, while outside I saw the fiery evening sky. It was by no means fully dark but the multicoloured smoke from the Pernis refinery drifted past against the dark blue.

Dozens of people were standing in the hall with flowers, even though it was only a quarter to seven and the visiting hour did not start till seven. All at once it dawned on me that at that moment healthy people all over Holland were waiting like that for the beginning of the visiting hour. It seemed as if mankind were divided into the sick and the waiting, and that I, through some lucky stroke of fortune, was still numbered among the waiting but that I myself should shortly be ill. It was almost as though that disheartening waiting, however camouflaged it might be by wild daffodils, brought the illness closer. A man was wheeled past on a stretcher, as white as the edge of a seagull's wing, moving his arm in his striped pyjama jacket as though he were steering, while a spirited little nurse tripped along behind the stretcher as if it were a pram.

"Ages to go yet!" she called out and an ill-humoured rumble went through the waiting crowd.

A ward-sister appeared at the end of a dark corridor and lifted her hands as though she were about to be crucified. "You can come in on the dot of seven, no earlier!"

She had already vanished again into the gloom. I stared at the growing crowd of visitors, realizing that just like me they had all come too early because they did not wish to be late when visiting a sick relative. Every now and then an agitated nurse would stride through the people with impatient swimming motions.

I was astonished that there should still be so much traffic outside on the motorway. Every Dutchman, it seemed to me, was bound to be waiting in the entrance hall of some hospital or other, whether carrying flowers or fruit or not, for in this hospital alone several hundred people were gathered. Then all at once I heard the deep sigh of a thousand throats: the big hand of the clock in the hall had jerked to twelve and as the noisy voices died away there arose such a strange, dull noise that at first I did not know what it was. It was not until I began walking myself that I realized it to be the sound of thousands of footsteps on the concrete: a sound that gathered force as we ascended the stairs and then ebbed away again in the corridors.

I walked behind my mother, following dozens of other people, towards one of the dark corridors in that vast labyrinth. Having visited my father three times already, my mother had some idea of the way and only got lost twice. First of all we found ourselves by mistake in the lung patients' ward and then, thinking we had reached the right room, we opened a store-cupboard out of which clattered three buckets and two scrubbing brushes. But the sound was lost in the thundery rumble of the reluctant footsteps and we did not even try to stuff the brushes back into the cupboard but dashed off as fast as we could, bumping in the process into a stretcher being pushed in zigzag fashion along the corridor between the visitors.

When we reached the room where my father was lying I did not see him. I saw six beds with six men in six pairs of striped pyjamas. I was on the point of leaving. For as long as I had known my father he had never worn pyjamas, just as he had never eaten cheese or yoghurt. He always slept in a pair of long white underpants and a cast-off blue shirt. But before I could leave he called out:

"Mart, can't you see me?"

"Are you wearing pyjamas?" I asked in astonishment, even feeling a little cross.

"Yes, they're the rules here. Well, so you've come at last. I could easily have been dead and buried by now and you stuck out somewhere in Drente without our knowing where — you left us no address, no telephone number, you really are a prize idiot."

"Hanneke's father and mother knew where we were."

"Yes, they did, they did of course; and we of course didn't. Why shouldn't we be told? Don't we count? Or is your father-in-law ill? Well, then! Your mother in a tizzy, no one knows the whereabouts of my eldest stinker and here I am with six bottles of blood stuck into me. Yes, I was nearly a goner yesterday — could have been buried just like that in the third-class rental grave I dug myself the day before yesterday. After that dreadful examination — they turned me right inside out — something inside me burst and I nearly bled to death. And you nowhere to be found! Six bottles of blood, as big as this."

He proudly indicated the size of the bottles with his hands.

"Half litres?" I asked.

"At least! I think they must have been whole litres."

"That's impossible: people don't have more than five litres of blood and that would have meant you had six litres."

"Well, in that case they replaced all my blood yesterday and gave me a bit extra. I've got new blood from tip to toe and I can feel it too — I'm as frisky as a new-born foal and keep eyeing the young nurses. Do you know what they love?"

He suddenly withdrew his leg from under the sheet. On his still youthful foot there was an enormous bulbous lump, which had scared me since infancy. Around the lump there was a double circle of small hairs but the lump itself was hairless, rather like a small skull that had gone bald prematurely.

"They all want to see it," my father said proudly. "Even doctors have been to have a look at it, and the nurses stroke it with their fingers and ask: 'How did you get it?' From wearing clogs, I tell them, and show them my other foot at the same time. They've already asked me: 'Can we cut off a little slice to examine it?' and I told them: 'If I die here, which is quite likely because you treat me like a pig — even any of Ai Kip's pigs used to get better treatment than here; we even used to show more kindness to useless old goats than you do your patients — then you can cut off the lump and see what's in it.' "

"I can see you're getting on like a house on fire," I said.

"You think so, do you? Well, they think I'm a spoiled old bugger because I'm used to getting my warm milk on time at home and here I don't get it — here I have to plead and beg for a little mug of warm milk even though, as I told one of those young nurses this afternoon, they've got an entire maternity ward where they have milk. And damn me if they can't spare a drop. 'Would it be so much trouble to prepare an extra bottle,' I said this afternoon to the sister, 'and to bring it here? I can take the teat off myself if necessary. Whatever do you do with all that milk?' I asked her. 'Do you by any chance make your own cheese? You'd think so from that wilted rubbish they bring you on a piece of bread. For heaven's sake bring me some warm milk: it's what I'm used to at home and if I don't have it I get racked with stomach pains.' 'What you're used to at home is none of our concern,' said one of those whipper-snapper nurses. 'Here you must abide by the rules of the house.'"

"That's enough, Pau," my mother said. "I've brought you some warm milk and will bring you some every afternoon and evening from now on."

"Jolly good. Go and make sure" (this to my brother-in-law) "there's no nurse coming — better stand guard at the door, and if you see one coming just call out Exodus 3 verse 8 and I'll know what's up and stick the milk under the blankets."

My mother produced a thermos flask and my father drank the warm milk he needed so badly. When he had consumed it he returned to the subject of the six bottles of blood.

"Do you really think they will have replaced all my blood?" he asked. .

"Six bottles. I'd think that was three litres. Not the lot, but most of it," I said.

"It must have been a young chap's blood — a high-spirited fellow with the bit between his teeth."

"It might have been a woman's blood."

"Oh, no, out of the question. I would have noticed that. No, they wouldn't give Pau Hart old wives' blood, no, no, no."

"So they'll operate tomorrow?"

"Yes, tomorrow at nine o'clock; I'll be the first. The doctor treating me, one of those darkies, a Malay, was here a moment ago. 'You've got a fine body for cutting up,' he said to me. Decent chap, much better than that specialist who examined me. What a brute he was! Sick as I

26

was, he made me swallow all sorts of muck and be photographed and he pounded my stomach like Piet van Dijk, that vet in Maasland who sometimes used to do the same thing to a pregnant cow, and you could usually pull the calf out dead afterwards. 'It will be quite a major operation,' the Malay said to me, 'but don't get worked up: you're still young and otherwise fit, with a heart like an Oldenburger and a pair of lungs like the bellows of a Mannborg.' "

"Did he really say that?"

"What?"

"About the Mannborg?"

"It's possible he mentioned some other make of harmonium, but he certainly used the word bellows."

He paused for a moment, chuckled quietly to himself and, sitting up, drew aside the curtain next to his bed.

"Just take a look at who's lying next to me."

I peered in the semi-darkness at the man in the next bed, who seemed very old. An old woman was sitting next to his bed. Neither spoke. They looked expectantly at my father.

"Can't you see who it is?" asked my father.

"Not yet."

"Have a good look — yes, it was a long time ago but it really is him. The three of us milked cows together. Surely you know now? Well, then, I'll give you a clue: that lady next to him — whom you know too, by the way — is his fiancée."

."Thijs Loosjes," I exclaimed.

"Exactly! Nice, isn't it? Means I've got some company here too. Do you remember my son, Thijs?"

I went over to the other bed and carefully shook the old man's hand, and the old woman's hand even more carefully since it looked so fragile that I half expected it might come off in my hand at any moment.

"Pau, Pau, what a big lad he's become."

"And already married too," my father said.

"Already married?"

"Yes, he didn't put it off as long as you did, but it's still not too late, you can still get married."

He turned towards me and said: "How old would you say Thijs is now?"

"About eighty."

"Not a bad guess. He's eight-two and in a year and a half he'll be celebrating the fiftieth anniversary of his engagement. He's in for his appendix. It'll be his turn after me tomorrow. Don't you think it's a bit silly, Thijs, to have your appendix removed at your age? You've got such a nice little house near the dyke — isn't it time to make room for a second person? A full ten years ago I selected a nice spot for you in Section E, plot A just by the rhododendrons. And here you are still alive! If I were you I'd nip off to the registry office — you're not spring chickens any more, it's your last chance."

"Now listen, Pau," Thijs said seriously, "I've been engaged all my life and it's suited me fine, just fine. Jannetje might have preferred otherwise but she learned to accept it and you remember what I told you long ago: people who are engaged don't die."

"You never told me that! And you know quite well it's not true. Why, just the other day I had a boy in the mortuary. Dashed himself to death on his moped. His fiancée on the back badly hurt too. Isaiah 1, verse 6, that tells you the lot. As I was mopping the floor after the doctor had gone — because quite a lot of blood had dripped on to it — he suddenly hit me on the head. It gave me the willies but nothing was up; his arm had just slipped off the slab."

"That story sounds familiar but it doesn't affect me at all. I don't have a moped and you can see in our case: two people as old as the hills but as fit as can be. All right, my appendix might be playing up but that can happen to anyone and will be put right tomorrow, and in a fortnight Jannetje and I will be back in God's holy tabernacle just as usual. We have never been ill, never argued, never had any worry over children, had every chance to converse when we went to church — yes, the Lord has indeed blessed us greatly."

I stared in amazement at the shrivelled-up little man who had already almost uttered more words than there were wrinkles on his birdlike head; while the old woman next to his bed, who was equally as wrinkled, nodded cheerfully and sometimes even lifted up a bony finger to add weight to her fiancé's words.

"At first I tried to change Thijs's ideas," she croaked at the end of his homily, "but I can see now that he was right. I have seen so much misery around me, in marriages and with children; the Lord spared us that and said to us: do not marry but stay engaged, and we have gladly borne the Cross of our engagement and will keep on bearing it as long as the Lord wishes to spare us."

"The Lord will spare us," said Thijs, "because people who are engaged do not die."

"No, Thijs," said Jannetje, "you know perfectly well that engaged people died during the war and that...."

"Doesn't count, there's no war now."

"But nobody enjoys eternal life."

" Engaged people do; they don't die."

"Just like you to be so pig-headed; of course they die."

"Nobody has ever tried for as long as we have before."

"No, people were smarter. To get a house you had to be married. If we had been married I wouldn't have had to spend my entire life boarding in rooms but we could have...."

"You're not going to carry on about that house again, are you?"

My father drew the curtain to but I could hear the voices of the two old people continuing to quarrel, and I scarcely listened to my father's monologue about the examination of his stomach. I brushed my hand across my forehead and looked outside, in search, it almost seemed, of more normal circumstances; but even the evening sky, seen from this height, was far from normal. The horizon was a blotched blaze. Green smoke divided the dark blue sky into two and red flames lit up the yellow shimmer in between. Underneath there was a forest of pipes, a freakish network of vertical and horizontal tubes that branched unpredictably, here and there emitting smoke which competed with the greenness for possession of the evening sky. But the green smoke was billowing out of the tallest pipe in such thick shafts that there was no real competition; the green smoke simply permitted the odd wisp to form a patch of yellow or green, and then only when those wisps were lit up by the eternal flames of the Pernis refinery.

I gazed at all those gleaming silver pipes but my father called me to order.

"Hey, master-dreamer, would you mind listening to me for just a moment longer? You're staying here tonight, I gather from your mother, and intend coming back again tomorrow after the operation. In that case would you mind going to the cemetery to switch on the motor? If it's not turned on, all my people will get wet feet in their coffins or might even float out to sea; and while you're there have a look at the pair of show pigeons — they'll be looking out for you. I've warmed Kippenek too. The keys are behind the Bible on the chimneypiece."

These words brought the visiting hour to a close. On the way back everything became normal again. I smelled the scent of spring, which was seasoned here with a pungent smell of sulphur, and two horses were standing motionlessly in a meadow in the way that horses do only in spring, their heads half lifted up as though listening intently to something that must have taken place in far-off times. Perhaps they can hear the neighing of their own kind on the battlefields, and are mourning their death in the spring twilight.

The Maassluis tower was already looming up, at once massive and slender. Tonight I would be sleeping at home again and I would hear the cheerful, misty sound of trains going past, a sound to be heard nowhere else; and from time to time at moments of near wakefulness I would hum in unison with the melancholy hooting of a ship's horn, while in the morning I would be awoken by the strident factory whistle of De Neef & Co. Why did I miss all that so much in Leiden? Why above all did I miss a harbour in that city? Why was there nothing I wanted to do more after getting home than to walk along the quayside? I walked first of all to the mole and looked out across the broad expanse of water on which there was a mysterious rusty ship on its way out to sea. I could not see under which flag it was sailing; the distance was too great and the light had become too dim. But it was at least a real, seaworthy vessel, and there were real tugs and pilot-boats lying in the harbour and you smelled the salt water and the tar oil on anchorchains. It was all real, so real and tangible that you could almost take it in your hands; not as pale and waxy as life in Leiden. There wasn't even a harbour there, or a river with lights twinkling on the other side and a ferry-boat crossing soundlessly in the mist rising off the water, and the sound of men's voices on the bridges of ships passing by on their way to seas of which one had never heard. I walked along the outer harbour to the inner harbour and past the house of my parents' doctor, which prompted me to deliver an address to my father.

"There's no need to get worked up. Your time has by no means come — your father lived well into his eighties and even though he had a walking-stick when he turned seventy he only used it to grapple women with and to strike on the cobblestones when he lost at draughts, and nearly all your brothers and sisters are still alive and you are the third-youngest. True, your eldest brother died, but that was an accident. What's that? Do I still remember what your father said when they brought him home? Yes, you've related that often enough. When he was carried in your father said: 'Confound it, that'll cost me two hundred guilders a year,' because you all handed your earnings over to your father to the last cent. That was an accident; he was caught in a flywheel in the United Rope Factory. All the others are still alive. Aunt Anna is seventy-five and Aunt Riek already seventy-three, and Uncle Klaas is still repairing harmoniums, even though he's been drawing a pension for ages, and Uncle Nico still ascends pulpits to ever-dwindling congregations because the Independent Calvinists keep on splitting up into a few true churches, and Uncle Piet is still in the vegetable trade as always, pension or no pension. Uncle Rinus is still a bricklayer. All right, Uncle Maarten died at fifty-seven, the same age as you are, but he had lung-cancer which he got after his daughter died in that terrible accident. If anyone were to die it would be Uncle Job with his asthma, but even Uncle Huib, with his heart of gold, is in fine form despite his humpback. No, you really haven't got stomach cancer, even though you might think so; no, I know you didn't say so but I know that's what you're thinking because your father-in-law was admitted to hospital and turned out to have cancer of the stomach after thirty years of stomach ache and a winter like the one you've just been through."

I was whispering all that to myself as I walked along the deserted harbour lying there just as it always had, the streetlamps casting a yellow light like everywhere else but with blue edges and damp shadows. There was no greenery growing anywhere and yet you could feel spring coming because the smell of the De Ploeg flour-mill was stronger than ever as it drove away the hint of spring in the air. I walked around the basin and looked at the Great Church across the water and at its reflection in the water, and I thought: if I could just see that reflection in Leiden from time to time it would be enough. I looked at the green bridge and the old housefronts. I just stood there looking and meanwhile something was gnawing away inside me, making me feel I would have to give up all those sparkling housefronts and the oily water if my father were to die. Because it had not been to him but to myself that I had been mumbling just then; I had wanted to exorcize not his but my own dark premonitions. Why was I so sure he was suffering from stomach cancer? Because had had had an internal haemorrhage after the examination? True, cancer could cause something like that, by attacking a blood vessel until it suddenly burst; but a stomach ulcer could have the same effect. And my father had been skittish, cheerful and rebellious, and had even thought of his work, asking me to switch on the motor to keep down the groundwater level at the cemetery. Surely one would not think of something like that if one were really suffering from cancer at an advanced stage?

In the basin a small boat chugged past with yellow tanks on its deck that appeared to stay behind in the reflection in the water, and further along a solitary man rowed under the bridge. I said to myself: "If that man in the rowing-boat emerges from under the bridge before the Shell boat rounds the corner, my father has not got cancer." The man in the rowing-boat was first. I breathed a sigh of relief but all the same the absurd competition did not provide me with sufficient certainty. Two seagulls were each perched on a mooring-post and I muttered: "If the one on the left flies up before the one on the right my father hasn't got cancer." But they did not fly up, but remained huddled on their posts. I clapped my hands, but they did not rise. I clapped again, but they remained transfixed where they were. I picked up a pebble and threw it at the gull on the left but it did not budge.

Not until tomorrow would I know what I had to face. Tomorrow they would cut him open and then it would be incontrovertibly clear whether or not he was condemned to die in the same terrible way as my grandfather. Walking on the dyke I looked round once more at the harbour and the Great Church. The hands of the clock glowed red in the gloom and far in the distance I heard the whistle of a coaster on the point of sailing. For a moment the happy feeling I used to get returned — thank goodness you're not sailing too — but it subsided because death seemed so near, so much in my father's reach.

3

The striped paths

First thing the next morning I proceeded to the cemetery with the enormous bunch of keys I had discovered in an old bowl behind the Bible on the mantelpiece. I walked along the entrance lane to the double gates between the undertaking parlour and the mortuary. At first I could not identify the key and heard a finch call three times before I found it and could open the gate. I shut it behind me to prevent others from following and walked along the path beside the ditch that separated the cemetery from the railway where it led to the section with chestnut trees. Few people had used the paths since Sunday, for here and there I could still see the lines my father always made on the paths on a Saturday morning. He would draw a harrow behind him along the paths and took a pride in dragging it so as to produce dead-straight lines in the gravel covering the paths. Did he do that because it made him feel as though he was ploughing again? Why else did he add a rather pointless and not even particularly decorative pattern to the paths?

I looked at the old, ornate monuments on the graves in the first-class section. Everywhere the chains which my father had so often painted silver sparkled, connecting up the little posts in front of the upright tombstones and around the horizontal ones. In winter he used the paint to turn branches of alder cones silver, which he would then distribute among friends as Christmas decorations. On various graves there were circular iron holders on a bar, in some of which conical pewter vases had been inserted. The flowers in the vases were mostly wilted, for my father was not there to remove them. I walked through the rhododendron section with its scentless flowers and the wide path down the middle, and past the stately horizontal tombstones on the underground vaults, and I noticed how much the stones had been ravaged and cracked by the elements in concert with time, and how ivy and moss growing clandestinely among the rhododendrons had obligingly covered the cracks. If one looked carefully one could see signs of weathering everywhere, but most of all among the private graves in the first class, since they had not been cleared out since the turn of the century. Yet nature had largely camouflaged the decay. I reached the small clump of lime trees along the ditch by the railway-line. Their blossom was so strongly scented that I momentarily forgot even the deafening cooing of wood-pigeons. It suddenly brought to mind those extraordinary lines of Annette von Droste-Hülshoff in which she described how the dead stretched out and stirred beneath the grass, moving their eyelashes.

As I mumbled the first two stanzas of the poem, regretting that I did not know the other two by heart, it occurred to me that while it was called "In the grass" it naturally concerned a cemetery, and I imagined how the dead under the grass did indeed stretch out and stir and lift their closed eyelashes. Then I heard the wood-pigeons again and the dead time was gone. I looked about me and saw that all the fruit-trees planted as conspicuously as possible among the graves by my father's predecessor were in blossom. I walked past the graves in the second class and saw to my surprise that the plot in front of the tombstone decorated with a white dove was almost entirely bare. Where were the magnificent ornamental poppies that the son had cultivated for ten years in the plot in front of the gravestone? He used even to stand next to his poppies on Sunday afternoons during the visiting hour to prevent them from being picked by visitors. Where were his wonderful urticaceae, which sometimes rose higher than his mother's gravestone? All those plants must have been removed only recently, for although chickweed and groundsel had come up in the plot they were still little more than shoots.

I walked past the Jewish section and noticed how the sprawling pellitory flourished everywhere among the fissures in the stones, sometimes even covering them completely. The Jewish section was surrounded by a fence, behind which the cow parsley rose head-high in the sunlit bank of the ditch. Before I had reached the cow parsley I had to pass the gravestone out of which there rose a stone hand, which I had been made to look at so often as a child with the words: "See, that man's hand grew out of his grave because he used to hit his father and mother." I picked my way down the side of the ditch. Halfway down I thought I saw a large male newt in all its finery sunning itself in the

34

light, which was tinged green by the fine algae, and I could have sworn that a bright-red stickleback darted off and that the larva of a yellow-edged waterbeetle continued imperturbably to devour its already unidentifiable prey. But when I crossed the plank to the pump-shed built directly over the ditch I could see nothing but dark-green algae. I opened the shed with a key, which it took me two finch-calls to find. I switched on the pump designed to lower the ground water level so that the coffins would not float off, and while the contented and almost inaudible sound of pumping filled the room I shut the door behind me and walked across the grass of the fourth-class section to the chapel, where the old stone balustrades and broad stairs with shallow steps were just as weathered as the grave monuments in the first class, except that here ivy-leaved toadflax rather than moss filled the cracks. How the toadflax was blossoming! One of the balustrades was completely purple and I even had to be careful not to squash the plants when climbing the steps. The key to the door of the chapel was just as difficult to find as all the other keys.

I went inside and instantly felt I had become smaller in that imposing if not particularly large space where the sunlight shone in through the lead-lighted windows, conjuring up all sorts of different colours on the floor and benches and grey walls. If you walked about slowly in that space with its smell of beeswax, you could see constantly changing colours on your clothes: red circles gliding gently over your trousers, little yellow squares on the sleeve of your coat. I walked over to the big table in the middle of the chapel and sat down on the sole chair, which belonged to the minister. An old Bible was lying on the table just in front of the chair, framed in little green and red and blue patches of light. The Bible was locked but it did not take me long to find the key: I knew which it was, the smallest key on the bunch, even though it concealed itself between the broad keys to the undertaking parlour and the mortuary. I unlocked the Bible, placed my thumb against the golden edge and threw it open. Over the years I had practised the art of throwing open the Bible, for it is an old custom among Protestants to open the Bible at random to see what God has to say. But I prefer to know beforehand the text I am to hear; I like to guide the Holy Spirit. It was not difficult for me to open the Bible at the place I had previously selected while still looking for the key; the finest book in the Bible is in the middle of the Word of the Lord, and the psalm I wished to read precisely halfway. I had often read psalms in a soft voice in the chapel, since the acoustics in that space were such that you could have heard a child whispering yards away. One was forced to speak in hushed tones and as a child I had often thought the chapel had been built like that in case an apparently dead person should be brought in in a coffin. A person like that would only need to sigh and it would have reverberated like a roll of thunder.

I began to read: "He that dwelleth in the secret place of the most high shall abide under the shadow of the Almighty." I had to stop for a moment after the first line to allow the echoes to reverberate; they filled the entire room, up to the very ridge of the roof, becoming steadily softer, and it felt as though I were hearing all the echoes of my own voice in bygone days and as though all the psalms I had read out here were to be heard again, and I reflected how curious it was that the more I had become an unbeliever the more I had come to appreciate those psalms.

As I was reading the third verse of the psalm I heard a sound outside which I could not place. I went to the lavatory, where there was a small window of ordinary glass. It did, however, mean getting up on the seat of the toilet to see outside. At first I could only see the cow parsley, which from this vantage point did not look so tall, and the now visible blue shimmer of speedwell beneath, until I saw a small box sail over the fence, followed by a net and then another net, and another box. Somebody must have been standing in the dense undergrowth on the other side of the fence throwing all these things across, but I could only see his hat. It was not until the thrower emerged low down in the ditch where the fence ended, cautiously wriggling past the barbed wire, that I saw it was an old man. At the expense of two wet feet he reached the cemetery. He gathered up all his bird-catching equipment from the long grass and set off gaily towards the chapel. He did not look up, so that I could continue watching him unobserved, and I wondered what I ought to do. Should I try to drive him away? Or should I leave him alone as long as he did not catch any rare birds? But perhaps he had come for the pair of bullfinches or for the little owls that had been nesting in the rabbit burrow near the Jewish section for such a long time. The thought of the little owls made it all the more difficult for me to drive him away because I had myself always wanted to have a little owl that sits on one's typewriter as one types and flies up each time the bell rings at the end of a line. I decided to watch a little longer; the birdcatcher would probably be besieged by sparrows, starlings and wood-pigeons when he scattered his bait. He set up his nets behind the chapel. It really was a bit much: my father had only been gone a few days and there was a man carrying on as though he was completely at home and always caught birds in this cemetery.

Black-headed gulls came up to watch as the man carefully folded his nets over the sticks on the stoneless ground of the fourth-class section. When he scattered the bait, turtle doves swooped down everywhere from the trees and starlings (which I could not see but hear) settled in the gutters of the chapel. Sparrows filled the hedge along the side of the ditch and the ear-splitting sound of all those birds twittering away as they gorged themselves on grains of corn and maize even penetrated into the chapel. And perhaps on more delicate morsels as well, intended for the goldfinches or siskins or greenfinches or possibly even the bullfinches. For the moment, there wasn't a special bird to be seen on the sunlit grass among the daisies and the cunningly placed nets which, with a good tug, could be made to fall over the turtle-doves and gulls. Strangely enough I hoped in spite of myself that some rare birds would appear; it was as though I were that old man, and to prevent myself from identifying with him I had to keep on telling myself that he no doubt wished to catch those birds in order to trade them clandestinely and not to keep them himself.

Then I heard quiet footsteps at the front of the chapel; whether deafened by the noise of the birds or so intent on looking at the sparrows and starlings near the nets, the old man apparently did not, for he remained sitting calmly in the shade of the chapel, with his hands full of strings. I could not see who was approaching but could only hear that at least two people were drawing near with crunching though firm footsteps. All at once the footsteps ceased; they had reached the edge of the paupers' graves and were now apparently walking on the grass. I heard a smoker's cough and the old man in the shadows seemed at last to realize something was up from the fact that the starlings were flying up and that a blackbird emitted a cry of alarm as it flew to a rowan. The old man got up but it was too late, for on the suddenly sunnier-looking path leading to the fourth-class section there appeared two policemen who were both obliterating the straight lines drawn in the gravel. One of them had such a long neck that it seemed he did not even have a head. They drew near with implacable indifference and the old man smiled nervously and walked towards them, letting go of his strings over-hastily, so that the carefully folded nets suddenly collapsed, catching no more than a few wolf-spiders or slugs.

Then they were standing there, the two men in uniform and the bird-catcher with the hat he had submissively taken off straight away and which he now held in his left hand by way of a permanent greeting. Possibly they were talking to one another but I could not hear anything because the air was filled with the scornful laughter of the turtle doves. The policeman began taking down the nets, helped by the man who had put them up so carefully, and I heard the word "confiscated" before they disappeared with all the bird-catcher's possessions. The old man walked away with them but whether he went with them in the police car which I heard drive off a moment later I do not know. As I bent down to get off the seat of the lavatory I casually glanced outside. It can have lasted no more than a fraction of a second and yet the image that rose before my eyes appeared to last for ever: I did not see the tombstones or the plots or the green of the hedges but only the crowns of the trees in blossom and it was as though all that existed outside was an orchard in flower with white and pink and sometimes even light-blue blossom. I jumped down from the seat of the lavatory, went back into the chapel, shut the Bible with the smallest key, locked the door to the chapel and walked back to the main entrance gate. To open and lock the gate I needed yet another key.

That evening we were waiting in the vast entrance hall as early as a quarter to seven while a faint drizzle fell on the umbrellas of approaching visitors. Now that the fine drizzle was becoming mixed with the smoke from Pernis they might well have done better to place a handkerchief in front of their mouths than to hold an umbrella above their heads. It was our first visit of the day because my father had not been allowed to have visitors in the middle of the day — "What about his warm milk?" (my mother); "Do you really think he'd be able to drink warm milk after an operation on his stomach?" (me) — and so, not knowing what to expect, we stood gazing as the large hand of the clock jerked along. Nowadays wherever one waits there is almost bound to be one of those jerking clocks nearby — a timepiece that considers it beneath its dignity to move normally. For me waiting has long consisted solely of looking at an illuminated clock-face on which a black or red second-hand proceeds evenly until it reaches twelve — which is rarely shown — where it stands still for a moment to allow the big hand to spring forward. That almost seems the very essence of waiting: the tension at the moment when the second-hand stands still and you wonder: will the other hand jerk on? and the subsequent relief when it does. While looking at a clock like that at a station, an airport or in the hall of a hospital one not only realizes how right James McClure is when he describes life as waiting for the gaps between the waits but it also seems as though life has consisted and will consist of nothing but waiting, and that the gaps between shrivel up into emptiness and nothingness because waiting seems to be the only thing that counts. Life is pointless but so is waiting; and therefore, on the principle of two negatives make a positive, the two together make waiting seem purposeful.

I had tried that day to ring the hospital. The day before we had been told that we might ring after eleven o'clock. And so as soon as I got home, with my head still full of that one glance at the crowns of trees in blossom, I had picked up the receiver in anticipation, dialled the number and listened to the calm ringing sound no fewer than sixteen times and to the cheerful voice that, after the sixteenth time, stated the name of the hospital clearly, which was as well since it was the sort of voice one might expect to hear if one had inadvertently been connected to an Eros Centre.

"I should like to enquire about my father's operation," I had said.

"Which department?"

"Internal medicine."

"I'll connect you."

There then followed a long series of mysterious crackling noises, like the croaking of tree-frogs that have hurt their back legs, and I kept on thinking I had been connected and that there was an expectant silence at the other end of the line, for which reason I had repeatedly stated my name bravely to the tree-frogs. But at last there was a melodious voice at the other end:

"Who are you waiting for?"

"I'm waiting to be connected to the internal medicine department."

"I'll connect you."

Once again those mysterious zoological noises.

"Gynaecology."

"Oh, I'm sorry. I wanted the internal medicine department."

"I'll transfer you to the switchboard."

For a long time there were no sounds at all, not even crackles. Then the singer I had started with: "Switchboard."

"I'm sorry to trouble you but you connected me to internal medicine and I got gynaecology instead. Would you mind. . . ."

She had already connected me and all of a sudden, without my having to wait, another member of the girls' choir said: "Internal medicine."

"Good morning, my name's Hart. I should like to find out how my father's operation went."

"Who was the doctor?"

"What . . . how . . . what do you mean?"

"Who treated him?" The singing had become impatient.

"Dr Langemeijer, I think."

"Then I'll connect you to his secretary."

Then, apart from the tree-frogs, there had also been soft voices and hesitant buzzing tones. Then came the honeyed alto of the secretary: "What can I do for you?"

"My name is Hart. My father was operated on this morning by Dr Langemeijer and I should like. . . ."

"But then it's not me you want but the ward-sister of the ward he's been taken to. I'll try and see if I can connect you and otherwise I'll transfer you to the switchboard."

Bedlam then broke loose at the other end of the line. First there was some buzzing, followed by remarkable shrill tones, while all the time there were soft voices in the background; once I even overheard, "Is it raining where you are too?" Something whistled and then somebody appeared to blow through an oboe, until at last the mezzo-soprano of whom I had almost grown fond reappeared: "Switchboard."

"Yes, it's Hart here again. I'm still trying to get information on my father's operation and Dr Langemeijer's secretary has just told me that I should speak to the ward-sister."

"What ward's your father in?"

"Internal medicine."

"Yes, I'm aware of that by now, but which floor?"

"Tenth."

"In which wing and which class?"

"East, I think, in the third class."

"I'll connect you."

And a moment later I heard: "East wing, tenth floor."

"Oh, this is Hart here. I should like to enquire whether you know anything about . . . whether the operation went . . . how it went."

"But Mr Hart, patients are sent to recovery after an operation. You'll have to speak to them; I'm afraid there's nothing we can tell you. Shall I try to connect you?"

"If it's not too much trouble."

She had connected me. I had heard only three crackling sounds before the engaged signal came, followed immediately by the charming sing-song voice with which I had begun: "The line's engaged, please wait."

I had waited. And while I had been on the telephone like that, unable to help thinking of Annette von Droste-Hülshoff's dead love, dead desire and dead time, I had all at once no longer known why I was ringing up, so that, after a soft, cheerful singing sound in my ears, relieved occasionally by the mezzo-soprano who kept on chirping, "Please wait, the line's still engaged," I had involuntarily replaced the receiver and asked my mother: "What was it I was ringing up about?" She had looked at me in astonishment and I had dialled the number again and had luckily got another soprano stating the name of the hospital.

With a firm voice I had said: "Could you connect me to the recovery ward?"

"Recovery."

"Oh, this is Hart here. Could you tell me please how my father's operation went?"

"I'll just have a look on the list. Oh, I think he's already back in the ward, or perhaps not; I'll call the ward-sister for you."

She had put the receiver down on a hard wooden table, which had sounded in my ears like a gun going off beside me. I had heard distant voices and laughter, and redoubled laughter — what a cheerful ward that must be with all those reviving patients — and a sound like a cork being popped from a bottle and then I had suddenly heard a distant male voice say: "Why's this phone off the hook?", whereupon the receiver had instantly been replaced and I had been cut off.

I had tried twice more. The first time I had got the recovery department again, where I had been told that he had already been transferred back to the ward; and then I had rung the east wing tenth floor again, where I was told he was not yet back in the ward. At this, despite feeble protests from my mother, I had given up.

We were standing in the vast hall and did not know what had happened. We looked at the way in which visitors entering the hall folded up their umbrellas. One visitor had shut his umbrella as he was stepping into one of the compartments of the revolving door while someone else had given the door a shove so that the over-hasty visitor, inextricably intertwined with his umbrella, had tumbled into the hall. Ah, how splendid it would have been if the man and his umbrella had been carted off on a stretcher. But he extracted the umbrella ribs from the lapel of his raincoat and flung them into a flower-stand.

It reached seven o'clock and we wandered along the corridors. I had oriented myself expertly the evening before, but the previous day's knowledge proved useless. My father had been transferred somewhere else and we entered all sorts of rooms in which patients or visitors looked up at us blankly, shaking their heads. We were only able to find him at all by a lucky accident when I suddenly heard his voice roaring "ow-ow-ow-ow". We were at his bedside before the end of his screech and looked at the transparent tube that went up his nose and the opaque one attached to his arm and at the bottle hanging over his head and at his drowsy, dull eyes. In the four other beds there were four other men with eight tubes and near the window Thijs Loosjes's fiancée was holding his arm, to which a tube was attached. Loosjes was moaning softly; the four other men were moaning softly; but my father kept on crying out and his plaintive wailing shocked the people visiting the other victims, as it did us, although we knew him to be a bit of a coward and inclined to lapse into hyperbole.

"Pau, your milk," said my mother, showing him the thermos.

"I can't drink any milk now," he whispered, after which he instantly began wailing like a child being smacked.

"Such pain," he said, "here in my stomach."

He began yelling again and I felt ashamed. A nurse appeared in the doorway, frowning.

"There's no need to make so much noise, is there?" she said.

By way of reply my father bellowed something between "ow" and "pain", and I went over to the window in an impotent effort to free myself from my sense of shame and sympathy, gazing at the rampant profusion of pipes on the horizon. Clouds drifted along a darker blue than the evening sky, and between them the pipes cast a cryptogram of smoke signals. The last rays of the sun sparkled on the horizontal tubes, on the almost silver oil-tanks, and on the small stretch of river we were able to make out. Even the small gap between the buildings through which the waterway could be seen provided an impression of mysterious ships and swiftly vanishing tufts of smoke in pursuit of greater activity. I followed the pipes and tubes with my eyes; they were like tree-branches outlined against a clear grey winter afternoon's sky. My father kept on clamouring; there could be no question of any conversation. Nor did people talk at the other beds. Only Thijs Loosjes and his fiancée were conducting a conversation, she in a whisper and he by means of his thin tube. When she asked:

"Thijs, will you promise we'll get married once you're better again," the tube began to shake "No".

My mother sat at my father's bedside and held his hand. I leafed through the exercise book next to his bed which contained a record of blood-pressure measurements, which had been taken every quarter of an hour. Between nine o'clock and a quarter to ten two readings were missing. Assuming that his blood pressure had been taken at nine o'clock just before the operation and at a quarter to ten straight after the operation, the whole operation, including the anaesthetization, could have taken no more than three-quarters of an hour; and before I could even comprehend what that meant and feel amazed at the fact that he was back in the ward when he should still have been in recovery, I seemed to hear the voice of one of my friends, a doctor, saying: "An open-and-shut case, an open-and-shut case."

If that was true, what else could it mean than that they had briefly looked inside, seen it was a hopeless case, and sewn him up again? How should I ever find out? I slipped into the corridor, found the ward-sister's room, and asked her straight out if she could tell me anything about my father's condition.

"Sir," she said sternly, "we do not provide any information here. You should consult your family doctor, who will tell you all you want to know."

4
Dark evenings

Ten days after the operation I travelled by train from Leiden to Maassluis. As I was looking at the horizon the thought sprang to mind: ". . . and a deceitful distance ever moving slowly within him: like as the remorseless monster, Death!" I could not remember where I had read that, and knew only it was from Dickens and that it had occurred to me because the family doctor had said to me a few hours earlier on the telephone: "Yes, I've got some details now. Could you perhaps come to see me; it's rather hard to explain on the telephone. This evening at six o'clock; would that suit you?" It had been the second time I had rung him. I dialled his number for the first time the day after the operation, when he had told me: "I'll have to wait for the hospital's report first. Could you ring me back in ten days' time?" In those ten days my father recovered so unbelievably fast as to make me feel almost ashamed at my fears of a serious illness. A week after the operation he was home again, where he told his friends of eight bottles of blood and maintained that a hospital was just like a monolithic gravestone and informed them that apart from striking similarities between a hospital and a cemetery — "There's a first, second and third class there too" — there were also clear differences: "In a cemetery when the box is lowered they address you as though you're still alive; in a hospital they treat you as though you're already dead. In a cemetery everything flourishes like the Garden of Eden and in a hospital even the odd plant in a flower-stand looks as though its last hour's come."

The meadows looked shady and inviting. It had been warm and sunny all day, as though it were summer rather than mid-May. The scent of flowers, which made one so thirsty, hung in the air and even penetrated through the small open window of the train compartment.

What would I be told? And what should I do after I had seen the doctor? Go to my parents? If I did not go, someone might tell them: "We saw your son walking along the quayside only last night." But if, as I fully expected, the family doctor were to tell me, "Cancer of the stomach," I would no longer have the will to visit them. Or should I go and tell them what was the matter with my father? No; I would not be able to do that straight after seeing the doctor. For that I would need first to muster courage and, as far as I could, to distance myself from what I had been told.

Shortly before six I was walking under the plane-trees along Station Road. From the trees came the deafening sound of a flock of roosting starlings. Their droppings fell continually on to the road but miraculously I was not hit. I just kept walking and was conscious of the fact that the splendour of spring weather had rarely made such an impression on me as at that time.

It made me think of my father: he had always said that he had never known a more beautiful morning than 10 May 1940, the day on which Germany invaded the Netherlands during the Second World War. "I was milking cows at Ai Kip's around four in the morning. It was already growing light and the birds sang as I had never heard them sing before, and it was fresh and warm at the same time, with glistening dewdrops everywhere, while the new-born foal of the mare that had kicked me lame ran neighing merrily through the meadow."

Yes, I thought, it's as though each succeeding springtime I discover something new in spring and as though each year I've partially forgotten what it was like the year before and can only remember it when I am actually experiencing it. And it's as if there are still things you fail to see — things of which you fail to grasp the essence. For it is not only the scents, not just the soft, melancholy atmosphere, not just the dark, velvety, vaulted evening skies lasting till so late, not just the impassioned song of blackbirds as dusk falls; no, there are other things as well, on which it is impossible to place one's finger. It is, I thought, like being in love. When she is not there you cannot picture her face. If she is there, you recall it again and yet you cannot say what precisely it is that leaves such a strong impression. But then I happened to see the heads of some small coltsfoot by the side of the road that had already lost their clocks and I thought: this might well be my father's last spring.

When I reached the harbour the sunlight shimmering on the water almost hurt my eyes. The shadows were already full and deep. Apart from me there was nobody on the quay to hear how clearly the chimes of the church-clock sounded in the thin, warm air. The smoke coming from the funnels of ships inside the harbour was the only sign of human presence and I reached the doctor's house totally unobserved at the last stroke of six.

He must have been waiting for me, for he saved me from ringing and waiting by opening the door as I approached, and led the way to his surgery.

"Well, do sit down," he said, shuffling his papers, rearranging a few pots on his desk, shifting a lamp, and lifting up his chair and putting it down again; and each action said more than the clearest exposition could have done. I suddenly felt sorry for him; how difficult it must be to impart tidings of death.

He sat down.

"Your father," he said.

He stood up again, walked over to a wastepaper basket, threw in an imaginary ball of paper, and reddened, apparently because he himself realized he was executing a motion in a vacuum.

"I'll look up the report," he said. "Well, no, it's not necessary, really. You're a biologist, aren't you? I suppose you know all about the pancreas?"

He wandered through the surgery. He was a friendly-faced middle-aged man; he did not have his white coat on.

"What do you know about carcinoma of the pancreas?" he asked.

"I thought it depended where the tumour was located," I said. "If it's not in the head it can sometimes get better, at least if it hasn't spread."

"Yes, if it's not in the head."

"So it's a head of the pancreas carcinoma," I said.

He nodded. "Was that what you expected?" he asked.

"No," I said. "I had expected something like that because the operation appeared to have been such a quick one and because you said you could not tell me over the phone, but I thought it would be a stomach cancer; it never occurred to me that it might be a tumour in the head of the pancreas."

"Yes," he said thoughtfully, "it's in the head of the pancreas. What ought we to do now? Tell your father? He's such an amusing, cheerful fellow and still looks so young. You'd never think he was in his late fifties, looking as youthful as he does. I like your father, even if he is a bit odd and, if I may say so, rather tactless. But how was it he became so odd?"

46

"Well, I'm not quite sure," I said, "but perhaps it was because he was always treated as a bit of an outcast at home and called 'that oaf'. He was the second youngest or, rather, he was followed by twins, and those two boys were always sickly and received far more attention than he did; he tended to be something of an also-ran as the ninth child. Before he was born his mother is supposed to have said: 'I would rather crawl on my knees from Maassluis to Delft than have another child.' He began working on farms at thirteen because his father said he was too stupid for anything else. Later he worked as a garden labourer and was even a market gardener for some time but could not keep it up because he had to pay such a high rent for the nursery. Then he took a job with the local council, at first in the parks and gardens and later as a hodman-roadworker, eventually ending up in the cemetery, where he's been working for twenty years."

"Yes, he's certainly familiar with death and he might even know how ill he is; but even so I'm not sure we should tell him now. He's recovering well from the operation and he's lively and in good spirits. Do we really need at this stage...? I don't know, I don't know. I've come across youthful men of his age before, who went into their shells when you told them they were incurably ill, and languished away."

"From what I know of my father I think he would find it difficult to come to terms with being told he could not recover."

"Oh, everybody has...is really unable to come to terms with it....It is a great burden; nobody can really cope with it."

"Perhaps he himself will realize it soon," I said.

"Yes, a cancerous tumour like that grows much more quickly in a young otherwise healthy fellow like that than it does in older people. I wouldn't give him more than half a year to live."

"Did they see it straight away?"

"They removed a piece of tissue, which they examined. They also made another exit from the stomach — look, like this, they attached the duodenum to the stomach here, round the back as it were, since the normal outlet was completely over-run and obstructed by the tumour. That was why he was in such pain and couldn't eat anything."

He made a drawing for me on the back of a roneoed circular. How innocent and benign it looked on paper!

"The tumour also attacked a stomach artery, which burst during the examination; hence the internal haemorrhaging, which was nearly fatal."

Once I was outside again it was as though a sentence had been passed on me. Above me the sky was arched in an unreal blue and I had to force myself to walk towards the station. I would have liked nothing better than to walk around the harbour for hours or to have gone to the Heads to watch the passing ships. That might be the best way of coming to terms with it: the fact that my father was to die from a carcinoma of the pancreas, that his death would be preceded by terrible suffering; and that, apart from the doctor, I was the only one to know and it appeared better to keep it to oneself as long as nothing seemed to be wrong. But at the same time I knew that even if I were to walk for hours on end about that sunny, shady harbour deprived of all greenery it would not help and that no ship, however large and however quickly it might be going out to sea, could take away the dull oppression in my chest. I walked beneath the plane trees, saw the overblown shepherd's purses and the silverweed, which had already been trampled underfoot, and with each step I took I not only drew nearer the station but also to the house of my father and mother, who would by now be sitting peacefully at dinner and perhaps had already reached the stage of reading the Bible. I could not bring myself to go straight to the station. I went to the street where my parents lived and walked to their house.

Once at the house I stopped, took a few more paces and peered cautiously past the lace curtains into the room. They were just folding their hands and shutting their eyes to say grace after the meal. I heard my father say the prayer in a loud voice: "We thank Thee most earnestly for these Thy abundant mercies, for many eat the bread of sorrows; but suffer our souls not to cling to this passing life but to abide by Thy commands that we might at last live eternally with Thee." I did not hear the amen, for I had already stepped back. The sight of them sitting there — and how peaceful and untroubled it had all looked — stayed with me vividly for a long time. The sunlight on their closed eyes and folded hands had been tempered by the Japanese cherry in blossom in the garden behind the house. One would have thought they had only just been married and had no children, and it was as though the doctor's story could only be an error because they had always been there, as long as I could remember, and it was inconceivable that one day they would cease to exist.

From the train I could see out over the cemetery where my father had told me he would start working again soon. There too it was sunny and peaceful; the shadows were static, the sun appeared to stand still like Gibeon, and between the undertaking parlour and the mortuary the moon hung palely against the light sky, while among the gravestones blackbirds and thrushes were looking for food and nesting materials.

In the first few days after the visit to the doctor, it was, above all, the image of my father and mother saying grace that managed to banish the dreadful thought that he was to die of cancer of the pancreas. But the image lost its power. I did, it is true, still see it before me, and ever more brilliantly, with more sunlight and more flowers on the Japanese cherry; but it became detached from the thought of cancer and slipped steadily into the past while that thought seemed particularly directed towards the future.

To my own surprise I noticed that I began to seek out friends of both sexes whose fathers had recently died. But I turned out not to possess any such friends. Where a father had died it was very long ago and often after a period of discord and hatred between the father and the son or daughter I happened to know. The fathers even of older friends were still living: the eighty-year-old father of my piano teacher would be standing in his son's garden, trimming the greater periwinkle, when I came for lessons, and the amiable father of my erudite ethology tutor still walked past our house daily without a stick on his morning constitutional, closer to ninety than eighty. After having seen the doctor I would dearly have loved to speak with someone who had lost their father fairly recently, but it proved impossible to find such a semi-orphan. I was surprised at my own reaction: what did I expect from such a conversation? Encouragement, comfort, support? I did not know what I wanted; nor did I know why I always tended to doze off after the evening meal and to dream of somebody who was tottering along the street unable to find so much as a wall or lamppost to lean against.

I was conscious of the fact that I was searching for support not just out of sorrow but also out of fear. My father, I realized then, had always stood between me and death, both because he was so strong, so fearless and so undaunted, and by virtue of his profession. As long as he was not dead I could not die, but if he should die I would be next in line. It did not matter whether next would be straight away or after many years: it was next. If he died the only person between me and death would be eliminated. True, I had always known that I too should die — or at least I had known that since the disenterment I had witnessed, because before then I had been convinced that Jesus would soon return on heavenly clouds; but, even after the disinterment, death had remained very distant and harmless. But once your father has to die it is like taking a giant, decisive step towards death. The distance between you and death is abruptly halved. Before then, and even earlier than the disinterment, I had taken steps in the direction of death, all of which had been related to my father. When our neighbour, Kraan, died, I had fled from death to find my father. And during the winter of 1963 I could not help thinking all the time of the man who had told my father he would take his own life once the ground had thawed. But this was the most decisive step: the death of my father. No, he had not died yet, but in my thoughts he was already so committed to dying that in my dreams I kept on walking along deserted streets after a funeral and seeing coming round the corner one of those men who still existed in my earliest boyhood and who were called *aanzeggers* — undertakers' men who bore the bad tidings of death from house to house.

Every evening I had to resist the impulse to ring my parents' number — it would only have alarmed them if I had rung each evening — because I wanted each time to confirm he was still alive: so dead did he seem to me. And when from time to time I did ring up and heard his voice, it was though I were speaking with someone who had already died. Ringing up proved, moreover, to be a difficult task. I had to be chatty and cheerful, which was difficult enough as it was but was made even more difficult when he kept on asking me what I thought about the operation:

"I can't help thinking something's wrong with my stomach," he would say.

"Why?"

"I don't know; I can eat what I like again and have no pain, but still I'm uneasy. Have you got around to ringing up that Langemeijer?"

He believed that was a simple matter for me, assuming that all academics were more or less on personal terms and addressed each other by their first names, and that for me to ring up his surgeon would be like ringing up a good friend. For that reason I said on one occasion: "He told me the same thing as the GP: that they made another outlet for your stomach because of an ulcer near the usual outlet."

"And what about those eight bottles of blood then?"

"An artery burst during the examination."

"Well, I expect it's all true but I'm still uneasy, precisely because I haven't got a scrap of pain any more. If it were still smarting a bit I would think: 'That's a left-over that's hasn't healed yet,' but now everything's in such good shape I don't trust it."

And then the receiver was put back, my line with the realm of the dead was cut, and I sat for a long time gazing ahead of me in bemusement. Was I right in not telling him? Did one have a right to know what was wrong? Would I myself want to know if I were condemned to die? I had no answer to the latter question. One moment the thought that another person would lie to me or conceal the truth on that point would drive me close to fury; while the next I would see in my mind's eye how I, as yet ignorant and seemingly healthy, would revel in the sunlight on my closed eyelids when I was eighty years old and incapable of doing anything but sitting in a chair in the garden in the sun, with a tumour in my body of which I did not, thank God, as yet know. I did not know what I ought to do — speak or remain silent — and I knew even less how I should have spoken if I had opened my mouth. Blurt out as he would have done: "You've got cancer of the pancreas and it's already so advanced you won't see out the summer. You might not even last until your birthday." That birthday was tremendously important to him; on that day he would become a year older than his brother who had died of lung-cancer. But while he might have been able to say something like that to someone, I knew that I could not. Very carefully then — in stages? I did not know, I could not do it, I put it off, and thought: "If the first signs of cancer appear I can still tell him. But not just yet; let him think he is well again, so that he can enjoy an unmarred spring, for as long as it lasts." But because I could not tell him and because there was nobody with whom I could talk about his death or the death of other fathers, it seemed as if I myself should die shortly — as long as I had to keep it to myself it was not his but my death.

That was the first phase: the saddest, and most depressing. Evening after evening I simply sat in the sitting-room, often as it grew dark and without turning on a light, while Hanneke studied yet another foreign language in her room upstairs. I was suddenly unable to read any more. They all seemed so absurd, all those novels and stories, which so rarely dealt with death and were nearly always written as though death did not exist at all. And even worse than my inability to read was the fact that there proved to be scarcely any music left that could offer solace or support. Bach, the great Bach, who had never let me down and who had always buoyed me up at the bleakest moments with Cantata 78 or 104 or the Air from the Third Suite for Orchestra, proved all at once to be far removed from death, for all that it had, through various texts, so often formed the inspiration for his compositions. *"Ich freue mich auf meinem Tod"*. Oh, no, wrong, untrue; one does not delight in one's death, not even as a faithful Christian. And naturally one does not delight in the death of someone one loves. Did I love my father? I had never asked myself that, at the most asking myself once as a small child whether, in line with the Bible's teachings, I loved God more than my father. Did I love my father? Not until then, in that spring, did I ask myself that question. I could well understand that others did not like him, because he was frequently rough and hard, and then suddenly sentimental with copious tears; occasionally he could be spiteful and could say the most incredibly coarse things. On one occasion he had shocked Hanneke deeply when he had seen our bedroom and she had happened to overhear him observe to me: "Well, so that's your action chamber is it; is that where you shoot your load?" But precisely because I could understand so well why certain other people did not like him, I liked him all the more, almost by way of compensation, for he was after all my father, and I had looked up to him as a child and had been scared to death when he had kicked me through the room in a wild rage shouting: "I'll kick you stone-dead." Yes, it was my father, and I had ridden in front on his bicycle, and his alone.

And then: you do not like someone because he or she is nice. My father always used to say that of all the horses he had known the one he had liked the best had been the mare that had kicked him lame. Perhaps you even like those people best of whom you have been afraid and to whom you have looked up and who treat you roughly, surprising you just now and then, perhaps once a year, with a mark of affection. My father had always treated me with a certain amount of contempt: "You're one of those real stalwarts, letting the whole world trample over you; you could be at your last gasp and you'd let someone snatch the last piece of cheese off your plate without protesting. Are you really a son of mine? Surely not, such a half-baked, friendly fellow. Why haven't you got any guts? A bigger milksop has yet to be born." He had said all that to me hundreds of times without my ever having been hurt; that was simply the way he talked and it only increased my admiration for him, and formed part of his complete lack of artifice, amicability or sentimentality. He always said exactly what he thought to everyone, something I could never do, and which therefore I always admired in him.

52

I preferred his cursing and grumbling to the rare tears of joy in his eyes when he looked at my reports from school. In an odd sort of way, I felt my spirits rise when he eventually began abusing me again after his operation and making scornful remarks — something he had not done for at least two years before the operation. At least that was my father: my spiteful, unfeeling and yet cheerful and witty father as I had always known him. But his truculence only returned in the course of the summer and could do nothing to cheer me during the spring of which I can still see before me the dark evenings and the still undrawn curtains and the moonlight. I sit in the dark sitting-room, with nothing at hand capable of diverting me or even of keeping me occupied, longing simply for some sort of solace, a sort of reassurance. I also see the little light of the amplifier in front of me and I see the gleaming, black surfaces of gramophone records glimmering in the darkness. During these evenings I tried out all sorts of music. One, only one, was there that came to my aid after some time and which softened and lightened the dull, heavy sense of oppression evening after evening. And yet, his music only rarely dealt with death. Indeed, it usually dealt with the scintillation and vitality of life — at least the music which appealed to me most and which I wanted to listen to again each evening, a far too short aria from *The Marriage of Figaro:* "Non sò più." Why did I wish to listen to that particular piece of music all the time? I could not explain it. Later, after a month or so, a second composer was added or perhaps it was not the composer but the voice that sang his songs. It was a voice which seemed to embody the very fear of death; a voice that forced tears to one's eyes when she sang: "O Tod, wie bitter bist du" or "In gold'nen Abendschein getauchet", and in which one could hear that its possessor would only live to forty-one and would die of cancer.

The only other thing that proved able to stand its ground and to help — and then only after the lapse of some time — was certain poetry. I read Obe Postma and Bloem, the former because of the wonderful harmony of his poetry, with its melancholy and yet blissful sense of coming to terms with life, while the latter's lines kept coming to mind during the day when all at once I no longer understood why I was doing what I was doing, because my father and I were both to die:

> And ever since the thought has stayed with me
> How greatly stiller death than sleeping is
> that living is a daily miracle,
> and to awake a resurrection seems.

But no matter how absurdly much Mozart meant to me that spring and summer and how often I recited lines of verse, usually even without thinking, it did not really help because I was constantly aware that Bloem and Mozart meant nothing to my father, even though Mozart had, like my father, enjoyed billiards. Let alone would he have understood why anybody should always have wanted to translate Obe Potsma's poem "Joun". It was as though I were mourning in a fraudulent way and were seeking a refuge because my father would act quite differently; he would open the Word and read in a stern voice: "Blessed is the people that know the joyful sound: they shall walk, O Lord, in the light of thy countenance."

5

In the gravediggers' shed

On one of the last days of spring our laboratory celebrated its centenary, which unexpectedly provided me with a free day. The evening before, as I was once again listening to Mozart by the steady glow of the amplifier's pilot light, it occurred to me that this might be my last opportunity to see the cemetery in spring with my father there. And so the next morning I rode off at the break of day on my racing bike. There was such a brisk north-north-east wind in my back that I sped along like a scooter over the towpath along the Rhine-Schie Canal. March flies gleamed on the cow parsley in the verges along the water, and late-flowering marsh-marigolds still stood out colourfully here and there in the fens on the other side of the narrow path. Even as I cycled along I seemed to leave the profound despondency of the past few days behind me in the timeworn university town — the ducks quacked brightly; the great black-backed gulls that had come so far inland flapped their wings jauntily. On the wings of the wind I sailed past the villas in Leidschendam, through the town of Delft, past Den Hoorn, through the lovely village of Schipluiden, and there looming up already was the village of Maasland. It was there my father and mother had been married in 1941; there that my father had worked as a farmhand for various farmers, and there that he had been a market-gardener. The village of Maasland lay with its two windmills and two towers, looking just as it always had, with no multi-storey flats or ugly new buildings: a childhood memory that refused to slip into the past. I did not ride through the village itself but rode along Westgaag, past Mrs Poot's allotment, where my father had worked for so many years, and felt surprised that all those old farms hadn't tumbled down yet and that marsh woundwart should still be growing at the water's edge despite all the weed-control. At the old Toll Gate I took the path to the Weverskade. I would so have liked to have ridden over the dyke once more, but it no longer existed and the old tin shed had gone and Maria's house too had been pulled down. Why should that always be so distressing — the disappearance of odd spots and buildings from one's youth, even though they were decidedly ugly? I flew through Maassluis and reached the General Cemetery towards ten. Near the gate there was an old man whom I knew vaguely — what was it about him? I chained my bicycle to a wooden post supporting a young elm, and the man came bustling up.

"Well, young sir, you've come to visit, have you?" he asked.

"Yes," I said.

"I expect you're rather a stranger here?"

"Well, less than you might think."

"I've never seen you here before and I've been coming here for quite a few years — just call me Cor, that's what my late father always called me too; just call me Cor, and if you think that's too short Cornelis is fine too, and if that's too long Nelis will do as well. Shall I show you around the cemetery a bit — I know where most of the graves are, I know my way about here you see. Been following what goes on here since I retired and I retired in 1956, so you'll understand...."

At first I though he was one of those old men who traditionally hung about the entrance to cemeteries in the hope of picking up a tip by showing infrequent visitors the graves of their relatives. Was this one of those old stagers, one of those cemetery vultures? I tried to remember when and where I had seen him before. It must have been long ago. Why hadn't he come in the meantime?

"You haven't just had a long illness, have you?"

"Now how did you guess that, young sir: yes, I lay before the pearly gates for three or so years, but they didn't want me yet, even though Peter was rattling his bunch of keys; they thought I was tough enough to keep going a bit longer yet. And that's why I'm back again."

Since it was impossible to shake him off I walked with him along the path to the main gate.

"We'd better keep an eye out for that gravedigger here, young man; he's a bit down on me. But at this time he generally has a cup of coffee in one of those sheds there at the back. If we're very quick we can go round behind the chapel without being seen and past the Jewish section, and then we'll reach that big rhododendron bush over there and he won't seen us when he comes out of his shed. He won't hear us; the wood-pigeons will see to that."

The wood-pigeon chorus was indeed cooing at full strength, so that it was even difficult to understand the old fellow.

"What does he do if he sees you?" I asked.

"He chases me away; he must have chased me away a hundred times. Once he threw a shovelful of sand over me, another time he suddenly ran his wheelbarrow between my legs and once he followed me with a watering can. Nasty fellow. I don't like him, even if he is good at his job, I have to admit that; he looks after everything here as though it were his very own."

We walked past the green-stained taps near the chapel that smelled so strongly of copper weathering.

"Why ever do you want to go to the rhododendron bush? That's not where I want to be."

"That's where there's the best view of the cemetery — just you come along, young sir, I'll take you where you want to be in just a moment; I know my way about here. When they bury me they'll walk along this path and then they'll turn the corner at that wooden cross. I wonder who'll follow my coffin: I've got lots of friends among the old timers here, but then, it's usually me who's following their coffin, you see — so you'd better look out, young man: the people I know usually die soon!"

Why did that piece of information cheer me up? I did not know and wanted to think about it, but the man kept on chattering. "To me it's the most beautiful thing there is, a cemetery. It's so elegant, isn't it? So peaceful and delightful, especially if the sun comes out a bit, which it nearly always does — the sun likes funerals. Now today, you see, today the weather's not right for a funeral; it's too windy. One's to be buried this afternoon but I feel for him, I really feel for him. I'll see to it that I get buried in summer, when its sunny and windless and the earth can be turned easily. I wouldn't mind a small cloud — in fact that would be nice — but preferably no wind, otherwise it lifts up the pall and you can no longer hear the minister properly."

He paused for a moment and extended his arm as though he were greeting someone.

"Here lies Piet Vastenou — yes, he hasn't got a gravestone but I always greet him. It really wasn't his day when he was buried: it was raining and the minister had a cold and the coffin got stuck halfway because the machine broke down. Now that's what I don't like about these modern days — once you used to be let down on ropes, as is surely only fitting. My, oh, my, how I'd like it to happen this

57

summer."

"What?" I enquired.

"My burial."

"This summer, you mean?"

"Yes, I've been looking forward to it for such a long time. I live for nothing else — oh, if only it would happen to me this summer. They've still got horses, you see, you can still be buried with horses; it's a little dearer, but I've saved up for it. It's just a matter of how long it lasts — those horses are bound to go, just like the ropes. Yes, that's right, come along; there, now we're safe from that gravedigger, now we can at least look at my plot in peace. Look, look, there it is."

"What?" I asked.

"My spot. This is where I'll come to lie, if I'm allowed to experience it."

He proudly pointed out a patch of grass to me in front of a dark stone.

"My Cornelia's been here for thirty years now. It's a family grave, you see, and my son Cor's there too. Yes, when he died of pneumonia when he was fourteen — spat all his blood out in one go, he did — we bought this grave. The upper spot's for me, here just below the surface, see, and some space has been left on the stone. I've chosen the words: 'Here lies Cornelis Vlaskamp, died in the Lord. Luke 2. 29—32. Rest in peace.' Lovely spot, don't you think? Tucked away nicely behind the rhododendron out of sight of the gravedigger, with a nice view of the railway line and Key & Kramer. There's a train every fifteen minutes with every now and then a boat-train to the Hook of Holland, so there's no need to get bored. Well, young man, I'm glad I've been able to show you that. Now tell me where you want to be."

Before I could reply a harsh voice said behind us: "You again, is it, Vlaskamp? Bugger off before I untwist one of your legs."

The old man made off so quickly that his chances of being buried that summer suddenly seemed very small to me. My father drew near; he had not spotted me as yet.

"He was not alone," my father said to Mr Quaavers, his immediate superior, whose long legs alone were visible to me between the gravestones. "Hey, Mart, is that you? You didn't let that old bridge-keeper lure you here, did you? What a clodhopper you are; surely you know he's been going up and down for years trying to lure people into being shown his plot?"

"Just leave the old buffer, he's not hurting anybody."

"Where the buggery will that get me? If I let him in there'll be ten tomorrow wanting to display their graves, and the day after that a hundred. How do you think I can keep the place tidy if all those pensioners start turning it into a showroom?"

"Good morning, Mr Quaavers," I said.

"Got a day off?" he asked.

"Quaavers has got good news today," my father said, "which is not often the case with him. The entire third class is going to be cleared — we can get rid of all those blasted stones and I'll at last be able to roll the grass with the motor mower. Couldn't we heave out all those bloody stones from the second and first class at the same time? That's what they're going to do at the Catholic cemetery — they're going to shift the whole Piet Pastoor cemetery, and even asked me if I wanted to do it. Only with a drag-line and bulldozer, I said."

"Paul, Paul," Mr Quaavers said, "now we're standing here I suddenly recall that you were going to bury all those people who went down in the *Volharding* in that plot there together."

"Now look here, that boat went down in 1929. They were buried all over the place. Some of the graves have been cleared since then; only the graves of the captain and the mate and the chief engineer are left. How am I meant to find out where all those sailors are? The cook I just managed to find because they stuck a ladle in his coffin. But the rest?"

"You've still got the records, haven't you?"

"Yes, but it would be a mighty tricky business putting all the bits and pieces together again. Whoever hit on the wretched idea of burying all those castaways from the *Volharding* together?"

"Paul, you know perfectly well that it was planned in 1954 when they commemorated the twenty-fifth anniversary of the shipwreck. In 1954, Paul — and now, nearly twenty years on, they've still not been brought together."

"They're out of their minds! Fancy brining all those blokes together in one plot. Well, now, it would be a different matter if they still had their sailor's hats on underground, but like this it's madness. I've been working here now for twenty years, and during all that time they've been on at me about that damned *Volharding*. How am I meant to find out where they are? One day one of those chaps came along who could tell without fail from looking at their dentures who had been on board that ship. 'Where am I expected to get the dentures from?' I say to him. 'Dig them up,' he said. 'Fine,' I say, 'if you know where they are.' 'That's your business,' he says. 'How can I be expected to know?' I say. 'Surely there are proper records?' he says. 'Yes,' I say, 'the records are in first-class order since I began working here, but it so happens that before then they're a complete shambles. Vreugdenhil, who was sacked because he used to sell gold rings after clearing graves, as well as skulls to young fellows wanting to become doctors, and who made his son take back all the bunches of flowers laid on the graves so that the florist could sell them again, and sometimes again, and again — with them splitting the profits — that Vreugdenhil made a right mess of them. He used to run goats on the sly among the graves as well and his records just don't tally at all. All those sailors disappeared ages ago — they've been on doctors' mantelpieces for twenty years now. Really, it's a waste of effort.' But words are no use: they've got to be buried together, no matter what. They didn't get washed up in the same spot, did they? Whoever hit upon the idea?"

"All the same, Paul, you must try and get the job done. Before long, on the fiftieth anniversary, the plot must be finished."

"In that case that confounded chestnut will have to come down first."

"Why?"

"How am I meant to dig in the plot if I keep on striking those damned roots?"

"But, Paul, it's a splendid chestnut. Surely you can find some way around the problem. They obviously chose the plot because of the chestnut."

"They chose the plot because they didn't know what to do with their money. But the chestnut's got to go."

"No, Paul, I can't permit that."

"Well, it's dying anway; by winter it will be dead as a dodo."

"Paul, what a strange feeling you've got for trees. If you say, 'That tree's going to die,' it does too."

"Yes, that's gardener's blood."

"Just recently, with that poplar near the main gate — you wanted to remove it, and I said: 'Paul, I want it to stay,' and you said: 'It's dying anyway,' and, so help me, a month later it was dead. That's how it always is. But this tree still looks as healthy as can be."

"It's going to die without fail."

"Well, let's wait and see. I'd better be on my way; I've still got lots to do today."

He walked off down the gravelled path. My father grinned slyly.

"Paul, never anything but Paul, even though I've told him a

hundred times my name's Pau. But I'll order a good load of weedkiller; it's amazing how it works. You spread it out under a tree like that and in a few weeks it's dead. Well, you've got to with a fellow like Quaavers. Not a bad chap, all the same: he would never run you down behind your back, unlike my old boss. What the hell does it matter whose bones are lying in that Volharding plot? He didn't say as much but it was clear to me what he meant: I was just to stick any old bones I happened to have dug up in that plot there. No, it's true, nobody would know a thing but I don't want to do that: it's the real sailors or nothing. No deception; I'll have none of that. And yet that's what they want: to pull the wool over everyone's eyes so that the high-ups know nothing of it officially and can take advantage of your willingness to mess about with the dead to put on a fine show when the plot is ceremonially opened. Well, count me out."

Pushing his wheelbarrow he strolled past the third class, pulling out some groundsel here and there, and singing a stanza from his favourite song:

"But while she was playing at ball
She fell in the wintery canal.
Now sings she with angelic hordes
To the glory of Jesus our Lord."

He put down his wheelbarrow and turned towards me: "So you were able to leave those rotten rodents of yours for the day, were you? Beats me what you see in them. It's a pity you didn't go on to be a doctor, or a doctor of law. You might even have become mayor, and would at least have been a useful member of society. You're not going to tell me that someone who spends half the day looking at sticklebacks and the other half at rats is doing anything of any use. But then, on the other hand, it's always the same, always like that parachutist."

"What parachutist?"

"That parachutist they told: when you jump out of the plane pull the right-hand cord. Then the parachute will open. If it doesn't open, pull the left-hand cord, and it's sure to open. On the ground you'll find a bicycle against the wall of a farm. You can take that. Well, the parachutist jumps, pulls the right-hand cord, parachute fails to open, he pulls the left-hand cord, parachute still doesn't open. 'I suppose that damned bike won't be there either,' he said. And that's how life goes too."

We walked past the second class; once again I saw the vacant plot.

"Whatever happened to those splendid poppies that fellow used to grow?" I asked.

"Haven't you heard? He was arrested just before I went into hospital."

"Why?"

"He was growing some sort of opium and hemp and all sorts of other dope."

"What? No, I don't believe a word of it."

"All right, don't, but that chap was no fool. Everything grows like blazes here; if we could turf out all the gravestones we could have a market garden that would run on oiled wheels."

In the distance I noticed that my father's assistant was busy digging a grave.

"Are you letting Gaag did a grave all by himself?" I asked in astonishment, because that was the work he usually insisted on doing himself.

"I'm not yet strong enough after the operation to dig a grave."

"I don't believe a word of it. You look as fit as a fiddle."

It was true. My father hadn't looked as young and cheerful for years. His eyes sparkled again as they used to.

"Well, I'm still not too good; I'd prefer to let him do it by himself. After all, he's got to learn; he goes about it in a very muddled way, but I can't help that. And slow! Takes an entire day to do a single grave, no problem. Not long after I first came here I could sometimes finish two graves before lunch, and a child's grave into the bargain if I got really worked up."

"Surely you never dug special graves for children?" I asked in surprise.

"Well, in a manner of speaking, I mean. But I have to hand it to Gaag: when it's finished it's a neat job. By the way, what do you think of my stomach? I don't trust it at all. I don't feel a thing any more — surely that's not right, I should still feel some pain. And then there were those ten bottles of blood."

We had reached the gravediggers' shed. My father opened the door and we entered the oblong, windowless hut. As always the pungent odours in the shed conjured up images of the past before my eyes. I smelled the odour of Dutch gin, of pall-bearers after a funeral, of cigars, wreaths, palls and of the machine oil used to maintain the appliance. But above all I smelled the odour of all the little animals that my father used to slaughter in that little shed at Christmas for his superiors in the Municipal Works. Once again I saw before me the chicken whose head he had chopped off at a single blow of his axe on a chopping block, and how the headless bird had scuttled off through the open door towards the first class, leaving a trail of blood over three horizontal stones and not coming to rest until it reached a little angel on a marble tombstone, so that the statuette ended up bathed in blood up to its calves. I saw the rabbits, the geese, the chickens and the goat that had bleated so dolefully, and I smelled the soup that my mother had made from the rabbits' heads — our Christmas dinner.

Before my father could shut the door there was a knock. My father pushed the door open again so quickly that the person who had been knocking fell over in the gravel. It turned out to be the florist; I think my father had already seen him coming.

"Well, that's not the first time you've been lying on the ground here practising for when you're on the slab," my father said.

"You did that on purpose, you wretch," said the florist.

"How could I know you were coming? I suppose you wanted some old wreaths again, did you? Stick in a fresh lily here and there, a new ribbon, an arum that'll last another day and you've got a wreath you can sell as new. Clear off, will you. Leen Stigter gets all the old wreaths now. I don't want to deal with you any more."

"I'll give you two fifty for an old wreath."

"I don't care if you offer me five guilders."

My father shut the door and pointed to the uniform hanging from the rafters.

"They've given me a new uniform," he said. "Well, I hope I'll be fit enough to wear it until I'm pensioned off, but I don't trust it. I also got a new velveteen suit. Would you wear it, perhaps? It really is too much: here you are having studied for all these years, and could perfectly well wear a smart suit with a tie and hat, and instead you get about in corduroy trousers and a workman's jersey. Is that what you slaved for all those years? Well, slaved, it came easily to you because you inherited my make-up. What a pity you did not become a doctor or mayor. I wouldn't mind so much if you hadn't abandoned your faith. But that I find dreadful. I can't understand it; even when you were still at kindergarten you knew all the Bible stories, could recite the names of all the books in the Old Testament, from Genesis to Malachi, backwards, and now you deny your Saviour. If only you knew how you've grieved me! Even if you were a sinner and laid yourself down under every green tree as the prophet says, that would be better than now."

"Yes," I said bitterly, "better to be a faithfull SS ghoul in a concentration camp than to be an upright but unbelieving attendant in a home for feeble-minded old folk."

"We're all sinners."

"Rubbish. Nonsense. I've never met nicer or more honourable people in my life than my parents-in-law, and yet they're bound to go to hell according...according....." In rage I was unable to get my words out.

"That's right, they'll go to hell if they do not repent."

"If they do not repent," I said acidly. "If Hitler had repented at the last moment after he poured petrol over himself and set himself alight, if he had stammered out, 'Jesus, have mercy on me,' he would have managed to go to heaven while all those Jews he had gassed and who did not recognize Jesus as their redeemer would go, according...according....."

"No," my father screamed, "no, there can be no forgiveness for someone like Hitler; never, there can't be."

"There you are," I said, "now you're coming into conflict with your own faith, with that loathsome notion that there should be forgiveness for the biggest sinner but that a good person who happens not to believe all that clap-trap is eternally damned."

"There can be no forgiveness for a man like Hitler," my father repeated stubbornly.

"I'm glad to hear you say it," I said, "because it means that you too can see there's something amiss with that faith."

I wanted to say something else, but thought better of it. We had had this discussion so many times. Each time we would end up with Hitler, and with the fact that a person like that was beyond salvation. It was just that I always wanted to hear my father say that: a final vestige of common sense as yet proof against Christianity.

"Is that a new appliance?" I asked, pointing to the gleaming, rectangular apparatus hanging on the wall.

"Yes," my father said abruptly. "It's much lighter than the old one, which had to be taken by wheelbarrow to the graveside. This one can easily be carried — at least I can, you of course couldn't, being as weak as a kitten. All we need now is a new children's one and we'll be all fixed up."

He fell silent and stared at me, his eyes suddenly filling with tears.

"I just can't understand," he said, "how you became like this. You used to be a proper scamp, a real son of mine, full of life and not afraid of anybody. Now you've become just as lily-livered as your mother. She only has to hear a spider cleaning its teeth and she starts trembling so you can hear her heart pounding. And you're just the same; you'll see, the two of you'll end up dying from some heart complaint."

"You just watch out yourself! If you keep on smoking at this rate — a packet of shag a day, plus all the packets of cigarettes you're given here — you'll end up with lung-cancer like your brother and...."

I got such a shock at my own words that I was forced to seize the edge of my chair to help stop my body from trembling violently. My anger about our discussion of a moment ago vanished. My father saw my trembling, but concluded simply that I was too cowardly to complete my sentence.

"You've got no personality," he said. "That book by Bordewijk is a rotten book, but at least that boy, that James, has personality. You're just like Tom Pinch in that book you made me read because there's so much in it about funerals — you remember, with that woman who likes people so much she is even prepared to lay them out for nothing. Yes, you're that type, a real Tom Pinch."

"Well, you know what the Scriptures say," I replied. " 'Blessed are the meek: for they shall inherit the earth'."

"Right; once they're lying here in the graveyard having been pestered to death. But the Scriptures also say: 'Eye for eye, tooth for tooth, hand for hand,' and I stick to that."

And then his voice trailed off abruptly as though something terrible had just occurred to him. He looked up at me, bent forward again and buried his face in his hands. He wept.

"It's all my own fault," he sobbed. "I've made you like this because I used to beat and kick you so much when you were still little. I would come home after another rotten day at that wretched Mrs Poot's and I would beat you and kick you through the room. I kicked all the grit and personality and resolve right out of you."

I was used to these sudden cloudbursts of my father's, but on this occasion he sobbed in such an affecting way that I felt compelled to comfort him.

"It wasn't as bad as that," I said. "And no matter how you beat me, I still always wanted to go with you to the garden and the market. If I had really taken the odd blow you used to give me seriously, do you think I would still have wanted to ride in front on your bicycle?"

"That's what makes it so bad," my father said. "You were so terribly fond of me and yet I used to beat you, day after day."

"If you didn't keep on reminding me about it I would have forgotten it long ago."

"Because I used to beat you, you've become a Tom Pinch. It's my fault, my fault."

"Stop that crying, will you," I said. "You know what your brother Job always used to say to me: 'Your father is Eli, your father is bringing you up like Hophni and Phinehas.'"

"That wretch," my father said, "I saw him only yesterday. Do you know what he said to me? 'It's not until you have grandchildren that you really know what life's about.' Yes, he's always said that to me. When he became engaged — because he beat me, even though he was younger — he said: 'It's not until you're engaged,' and when he got married he said: 'It's not until you're married,' and when his first child arrived, he said: 'It's not until you become a father.' He did everything before I did. Do you know what I hope now? That he'll die before me too, which he probably will because he squeaks like a wheelbarrow that hasn't been oiled for several years. Unfortunately as a relative I won't be permitted to bury him myself, because I would have let him down with such speed that he thought he was in an express lift. But once he's buried I'll lie on top of the coffin straight after the funeral and place my ear against the lid and wait until I hear him say: 'It's not until you're dead.'"

6
The incident and the dream

Why should I relate how I deliberately knocked down an old man? I could easily pass over this part of the story; it scarcely reflects credit on me, and it is by no means essential for an understanding of what follows. Or am I just trying to persuade myself along those lines so that I can conceal the incident? If I am to relate it I must also say what happened before, which is equally unpraiseworthy. At any event, I think it arose from the fact that my father had compared me with Tom Pinch, even though Dickens's novel contained a figure like Mark Tapley. If only to prove I was no Tom Pinch, I began without any conscious intention to behave aggressively after my visit to the gravediggers' shed. In my mind's eye I can still see how I opened the door of our house one Friday morning and wheeled out my bicycle, bumping into an elderly person who used to pass by every morning, with a bag mounted on one of those frail trolleys constructed out of thin metal tubes, in search of stale bread. He always made out that he was collecting the bread to feed to the ducks, but I suspected him of eating it himself in the form of bread-sop. He used to ring the bell at every house and beg for old bread. If there was no response he would peer through the letter-box. He rummaged about in dustbins and ferreted in containers. And there he was now, gesticulating angrily with his walking-stick while he tried to disengage his trolley from my left pedal.

"Can't you look where you're going?" he asked.

"Can't you look where *you're* going — you saw the front door opening, didn't you?"

"Yes, but you charged out at high speed."

"Not at all, you weren't paying attention; you were already thinking about the ducks that don't get the stale bread you eat yourself."

He mumbled something and waved his walking-stick through the air. Each time he waved his stick he would shift his left leg aside, so that he assumed the appearance of a fan that was being opened and shut.

"You eat it all yourself," I repeated. "You make it into bread-sop."

"Quite untrue."

"And it's high time you stopped scrabbling through dustbins — it's a very dirty habit."

"What's it got to do with you?"

"Yes, and you rummage through the rubbish bin at the Café Pardoeza — I saw you only the other day — it's damned filthy."

"I was rummaging through it because my hat had fallen in."

"How did your hat happen to fall in? Because you were craning forward so much it couldn't help falling off."

He waved his walking-stick backwards and forwards at increasing speed. "What business is it of yours?"

"Everything, because you cart that rubbish all over the canal-side and tip over dustbins; you're like some old street-dog."

"If I were a street-dog I'd relieve myself here in front of your door, here and nowhere else, and I'd piddle against the front of your house until it stank from top to bottom; or no, I'd piss through your letterbox — haha, look out, young fellow, I've got you well and truly taped. Never got any bread for me, have you, you Scrooge, eat it all yourself.... This is where I'd shit."

With his walking-stick he indicated the precise spot next to the front door. I left him standing there, shut the front door and rode off, above all amazed at what I had wanted to say, and choked back as I rode along: "An old prick like you could only drip, not piss, and wouldn't get stiff in a hundred years." Why should I have been annoyed with myself at having failed to come out with that, and yet at the same time vaguely gratified that I had refrained from such nonsense? Had I been infected by my father's spirit? I thought about it as I cycled to the post office. I ended up at a counter with a queue that simply would not grow smaller. I recalled Bob den Uyl's law: the line you're in never moves, and if you change lines the new one immediately stops moving. So I stayed where I was, and my anger at the man with the stale bread cart and with myself increased. Why hadn't I been able to reply with a lighter touch? The line shuffled forward a little. This was not really the right time to visit the post office. Old-age pensioners came from far and wide just before ten for some trifling transaction and for the sake of human contact.

68

Everywhere I was surrounded by elderly people; I counted at least four in each line, and in my own row there were three ahead of me.

The one at the head of the queue left. Next in line was an old man with red-veined cheeks and a small hat that had shrunk more rapidly that he had himself, so that this article of apparel covered only the back part of his head.

"Sir," he began, "I want to transfer some money to my son because he advanced me some money, a long time ago now, for a Rhine trip, you see, and now, because it's been such a long time, I'd like to transfer the money to him quickly because my son tends to flare up rather easily, and I've just been told by my downstairs neighbour in our home — yes, I'm in the Vijfhoven old folks home; my son arranged for me to get in, I didn't want to go at first but he used to say, 'Gramps, you've got to leave here. This is a fine house for me, you've got to go to an old folks' home' — well, she told me that there was some way of doing that quickly, and I wanted to enquire...."

"Sir, you write the sum on a blue card, put 'express delivery' on the envelope, and bring me the envelope, unsealed."

"An ordinary envelope?"

"No, sir, of course not — a giro envelope."

"Oh, thank you very much, sir, many thanks; so 'express service' on the outside and then hand in the unsealed envelope here?"

"Yes, sir."

"Oh, thank you very much, sir, thank you very much."

"Next," said the counter-clerk, turning to the pensioner in front of me.

But the man with the undersize hat was not to be palmed off as easily as that. "How much sooner will he get the money then? It's urgent, you see, sir, because my son has told me, 'Gramps, where the blazes is that money?' Well, I didn't really want to give it back because he gave it to me for the Rhine trip and at the time I thought, 'What a fine lad that son of mine is,' but it might have been because he wanted me out of the way because when I came back all my things had been shifted to Vijfhoven and my son was in my house as proud as a lord. Well, now, I don't mean to be critical, but I was a bit upset at the time, which is why I didn't want to give him back the money."

"Sir, if you send it express delivery your son will get it one day earlier."

"One day earlier? That's hardly worth the effort."

"If you want to send it quicker still, bring me the unsealed envelope and then we can telegraph that the money's on the way."

But that was too complicated for the old man, who reverted to the first formula.

"So I should write 'express' on the envelope, should I, sir?"

"Yes, sir," said the counter-clerk offhandedly.

"Oh, thank you very much, sir."

The old man half-turned round; it seemed he was going. The counter-clerk had already taken a giro payment card from the next customer. But the old man stood transfixed as though struck by lightning and returned to the counter, asking anxiously: "Does it cost anything, sir, one of those express...express thingamys?"

"Yes, sir, there's an express fee of twenty-five cents."

"Twenty-five cents? And that saves one day, does it?"

"Yes, one day."

"Oh, thank you very much, sir. Well, if it makes a difference of only one day, I think I might as well send it ordinary mail; he's waited long enough as it is. Thank you kindly for all your information, thanks very much."

He turned away, and once more you could see that an idea was taking shape under the flimsy hat.

"Sir," he called out, turning a quarter of a turn, "if I send it express...that express...what did you call it?"

"Express delivery."

"If I were to send it express...delivery, what counter should I hand it in at?"

"At counter one."

"Oh, that's over there, isn't it? Oh, oh, yes, I see, and an unsealed envelope, isn't it, with that express...express business on the outside?"

"Yes, sir, I've told you that twenty times by now."

"Don't get impatient, sir; my son's got the same trouble. But thank you very much, sir, thank you most kindly for all your trouble. I should like to thank you most warmly."

And indeed off he went, visibly satisfied. Momentarily he turned round again, because a fresh thought had evidently arisen in his brain, but he pulled himself together and entered the revolving door, where he waited calmly until a customer entering the post office moved the door for him. During the short interval that he was shut in his compartment in the revolving door, he held his hat in his left hand and dusted the crown off with his right. He did not leave his compartment once he was outside but went round again, thus being trapped inside twice more. Each time he was released he put on his hat — only to dust it again when he was shut in again. I had plenty of time to watch the performance because the old man ahead of me who had to pay one guilder eighty-five made frantic efforts to extract his wallet from his trouser pocket.

"My wife put it in for me and then it always gets stuck tight — funny, isn't it?" he said to the counter-clerk.

At last it appeared: a wallet of such small proportions that it must have been lost rather than stuck, and the man opened it with trembling fingers and extracted a guilder. He inspected the coin from all sides and said: "You've got to be so careful these days; it's so easy to confuse a two-fifty piece with a single guilder."

Then at last he put the coin down, and I felt such an uncontrollable urge to stick a knee into him (because he was so small that I needed only to lift my knee to get him square in the crotch from behind) that I had to find some other release for my rising anger. By chance there was a lady behind me whose dog was draped over her feet in such a way that its tail was just next to my left foot. It was not a big dog (oh, coward!) and so I stood quickly on its brown fur. I could have been shifting feet: nobody could suspect it of being a frivolous first step towards geronticide. And while the bitch barked and yelped sporadically, the man in front of me had now got as far as a twenty-five cent piece. This too he examined as if afraid of tendering a strange coin by mistake, all but letting it fall on the floor to see if it were made of cardboard. There then followed two ten-cent bits and a long gap of rummaging, after which cigarette papers suddenly flew up out of the wallet as though some mysterious gust of wind had made a detour. With infuriating slowness the man counted out four five-cent pieces, of which he took back one that gleamed from newness or a night in Coca Cola, replacing it with another that was rather rusty. But the cents, twenty in all, took the longest. My anger rose and the dog went on barking, and then the man said:

"There, that's it, I think."

"Yes," said the counter-clerk.

The man disappeared and I was served, even overtaking the old man outside because he stopped to strike up a chat with a member of the Salvation Army at the door while giving him the sparkling five-cent piece; and once again the impulse arose to knee him in the back, just as I was looking down on his hat and thinking of my father's words: "There are two sorts of men: those who wear hats on Sundays only and those who wear hats during the week as well," and I thought: *That no longer applies; now only the elderly wear hats.* The thought did nothing to assuage my irritation. I cycled along the street, burning with rage, and thought about that dog. All at once I was not sure whether I had trodden on its tail to prevent myself from kneeing the man in the back, or because my father hated dogs. Had it been something more than just "redirected aggression"? I pondered on the question, or acted as though I were, and failed to look where I was going; and, as calmly and confidently as if I had been Mark Tapley, unconcernedly ran slap into the odd little old chap who always stood on the bridge near the post office and who used to greet me with the words: "Nothing to do again today, no doubt," or "Shouldn't you be at work?" or "Nice cycle ride in the boss's time."

He was lying on the road and his hat rolled away and was crushed beneath the wheels of a bus, which gave me so much satisfaction that my fury temporarily abated. As I helped the no longer waggish but deeply shocked man to his feet and hypocritically mumbled an apology, I knew that I was no Tom Pinch — at least not at that moment — but also no Mark Tapley: I was behaving as my father would have done, and the rage I felt was not my rage but my father's. But I also knew that my sense of rage was concentrated on this man and the old timers at the counter and the man with the stale bread because they were already older than my father would ever be. I knew that I hated them to the very depths of my soul because they were still alive, while my father was in a manner of speaking already dead. Who had given them the right to become older than my father? Why wasn't there, as in Trollope's novel *The Fixed Period,* simply an age limit which people were not allowed to exceed? Finished off, they should be, all those old-timers, the whole lot of them, off with them; I had only to see them in the street in their hundreds, or to hear their sluggish footsteps or to catch sight of a surgical stocking for the rage to well up in me again. It was totally uncreative rage: rage that gave rise only to swearing or to kneeing someone in the back. It was my father's rage on Sunday mornings when the bell rang and there was a Jehovah's witness at the door. My father would then open the door just so far that the man would stick his foot in, almost by way of reflex. And then my father would push the door to with all the power at his command — which was surprisingly great — so that the Jehovah's witness would limp off. But every now and then my father would come up with something better than such retribution. On one occasion he had opened the door at one of those absurdly early hours and had asked the two Jehovah's witnesses without further ado: "What does Matthew 27:5 say?" They did not know and my father made them look it up in their Bible. They read out: "'And Judas departed, and went and hanged himself'." "And now look up Acts 21:24," said my father, and they looked it up, when my father had pointed out the words to them: "That thy thyself also walkest."

But I got no further than jamming a foot in the door. I hated the elderly; and at a later stage even despised children, and would have liked nothing better than to throw large stones at dogs. There was no longer any question of listening to Mozart in the evening; that mysterious needle in one's inner compass, that registers one's problems so clearly by means of a preference for a particular composer at different stages of one's life, pointed to Beethoven and Bartok and Mahler, composers who normally meant nothing to me. But now I heard the aggression and sought to channel through music the sense of bitter hate I felt towards anyone living beyond sixty, while the malignant tumour in my father continued to spread.

My malevolence was so great that it even affected Hanneke. "Whatever's up with you?" she asked time after time when I had flared up gruffly or irritably at her or at someone else. She maintained it was because our holiday in the woods had been cut short.

"You need a change of scene," she said.

She believes that, no matter what is wrong, one will return cured or changed from a holiday. No power on earth can convince her otherwise. If she were a doctor her patients would all be in far-off health resorts; if she had been a psychiatrist she would have conducted her profession from the vestibule of a tourist bureau. An international train ticket is enough in itself to bring colour to her cheeks; when tired she can be buoyed up with accounts of lugging heavy cases about, and when she is catching a cold a glimpse of a rucksack does her more good than grams of vitamin C. But I do not believe in the power of travel and changes of scene. Nor did I believe in it then, for I would only take the source of my rage with me, and elderly people would be bound to cross my path wherever I went.

Even so there was one reason for making a trip, a reason of which I was well aware but which I was unable to express to myself, let alone to others. I was tired of waiting, and expected every day to hear from my mother: "Things have suddenly taken a turn for the worse with your father." But that did not happen. He became steadily healthier and livelier. As long as it did not happen I was obliged to keep my secret totally to myself, which had almost developed into a canker of the spirit from which, however strange it might sound, I wished to be released, even at the high price of the first outward symptoms of cancer showing in my father. The very fact that he was becoming more and more youthful made it all the more difficult. His cheerful lies made a mockery of my dark evenings with Mozart and the rage I shared with Beethoven. At the informal weekly meetings of the volunteer fire-brigade, which he had joined for the billiards, and at Uncle Klaas's on Saturday afternoons, he played with a verve and vitality that astonished everybody, now and then even beating Uncle Klaas. When I saw him he would give me an account of his scores going back for weeks: "Then I made a string of cannons and Klaas only shot four and then I finished off the game and you should have seen my brother's face."

I regarded it all as the lull before the storm, the final flaring up of a candle about to go out. I did not long for the storm, by any means; but I was unable to endure that inward waiting, which seemed so purposeless in the midst of so much health. For that reason I should have preferred to have gone again to Uncle Leendert's house in the morbid hope that there would be another telephone call from Maassluis putting an end to the paralysing uncertainty of waiting. But the two mysterious policemen kept me from tackling Hanneke about the woods, and she was keen to go abroad. It was at that time that a Swiss suddenly turned up at the laboratory who had done research with us before but who was now just on holiday. He told me with pride that he had bought an old farm in the Binntal as a weekend cottage, and he straight away offered me the house if I still wished to travel to Switzerland that year. After I had confirmed that the house was on the telephone, I arranged a date with him on the spot, since a house like that would be reminiscent of the woods. Moreover it had been he who had recommended that I read Jeremias Gotthelf, whose *Bauernspiegel* had made me think irresistibly of my father. I had even managed to purchase an ancient translation of the book at Lampusiak's. I had given the second-hand edition to my father to read. He too had enjoyed the book, so that at last, after all those years of quarrelling over books, starting with *Karakter*, here was a book we both admired. It seemed as though everything fitted neatly together and there in the

Binntal I would at last be able to return to normal.

We set off; the journey resembled the manner in which the old man had paid out his guilder and eighty-five cents. First there was a rapid and comfortable journey to Basle, followed by rather slower progress on the stretch to Brig. And there it became hard going: the rack-railway to Fiesch not only departed late but hobbled uncertainly towards the source of the Rhone. In Fiesch we had to wait for hours for the bus to Binn, and when at last we had reached the sunny market square in the village, it turned out that we still had a further five kilometres to go uphill to Imfeld, the spot where the cottage was, and which we could see in the distance as a disorderly collection of black huts. I lugged the two heavy suitcases uphill, and that in itself dulled my rage, giving way instead to a benign weariness. Once we had reached the huts it seemed as though I had never been angry and would never be angry again. Now it only remained to obtain the key to the cottage, which we had been told we could get from the Zumturm family.

There were no streets in the village; the huts were grouped around a little square, which was flanked on one side by a miniature church. Everything lay bathed in sunny desolation. A few chickens bustled about between the huts; a ginger tomcat stole past the wooden tub next to the pump, and a redstart's tail glistened in the sun on a farm gate. Farmers were cutting grass in the depths below; that was the only sign of human life.

"Would that be the Zumturm family?" Hanneke asked.

"It could well be. Why not go and ask? There doesn't appear to be a soul here."

Although I said, "why not go and ask?" to her I immediately set off myself. I walked along a narrow path towards the farmers and I seemed to leave the village behind me at lighting speed. The scent of freshly-cut grass penetrated my nostrils and my father seemed at once very distant and very close — for, long before I was born, my father used to cut grass and make hay. All at once I felt transported into his past, before his marriage, and as long as that had not yet taken place and I had not yet arrived there could be no threat of death. I walked along and the scent of the freshly-cut grass was so exquisite, while the sun transformed the valley into a Garden of Eden, that I became steadily smaller in the midst of those gigantic mountain walls. Here it was much easier to accept death, perhaps because everything was so green and smelt so heavenly; perhaps you knew nothing would ever change, since neither the construction of a new road nor the demolition or building of new houses could make much impression on those mountain faces covered with green pine trees. The village already lay far behind me; Hanneke had become a mere speck and a buzzard flapped slowly high in the sky. I reached a red-haired woman on a tractor.

"Are you Frau Zumturm?"

"Yes, are you Herr Hart?"

"Yes."

"Well, then, I'll give you the key."

She called over a small red-haired girl, gave her an enormous key and, as far as I followed the Swiss German and the Binntal accent, signified that she should show me the house. I walked back next to the surprisingly small girl. I had seldom seen such magnificent red hair and I was unable to talk to her, not only because I spoke no Swiss-German but also because I could think of nothing to say to such a girl. So I simply wondered, what would it be like to have a little daughter with such magnificent red hair?

In the village she pointed out a house to us, but as she was scampering back it turned out that the key did not fit. What now? We tried the key at a few other cottages, without result except that at one point we were only able to extract it from a keyhole with force, and so, once I had the key again, I walked back to the edge of the village. Frau Zumturm was coming along the path. She was dressed completely in black and looked like a shadow as she approached between the sun-drenched grassy slopes. There was a curious sluggishness about her approach. I felt sorry for her and wanted to run and meet her, but she waved that I should stay where I was. She approached without drawing closer, seeming to take hours over that short stretch along which I had dashed not long before. Beyond her the tractor was going up and down, now occupied by a red-haired youth, while everywhere red-haired girls and boys were cutting the grass with its profusion of blue cranesbill.

Then Frau Zumturm at last reached the pump and she walked quite normally across the square; she was not in any way crippled as I had imagined, but the perspective had been distorted by the mountain-walls and the sunlight, lending an air of slow-motion to her approach.

"I just realized that my daughter didn't really know which house it is. She's sure to have shown you the wrong one."

She showed us a house where the key did fit. It was a peasant dwelling with such absurdly low doors that even Hanneke, for all her modest size, was forced to stoop. I banged my head so unmercifully hard in the very first doorway that I was able only dizzily to admire the large stone hearth dating to 1601 in the living-room. I hit my head for three days on end, after which I became used to moving about the house like a quadruped — something that came more easily to me when it also proved easier to walk about in the valley on all fours. That way one's eyes were closer to the ground and there was less chance of overlooking some rare mineral. For we soon realized, not least because of the noise made by the scores of stone-breakers in the valley, that the Binntal was renowned for the presence of rare minerals. Not that we ever found one, but precisely for that reason I kept on stubbornly looking for them on all fours.

The first night in the cottage I had a dream that has since recurred many times. I can explain the dream's origins but it nevertheless always makes an overwhelming impression on me. It stems from a childhood memory: I am walking with my mother among the poppies growing on the embankment along the Nieuwe Weg, in Maassluis. It is summer and Sunday afternoon, and something has happened but I do not know what. Looking back I cannot understand why we were walking there, for my mother was afraid of poppies because they were poisonous and moreoever we never went out on Sunday afternoons.

Whatever happened seems to have been terribly important, but I shall never discover what it was; any more than I will ever find out what happened the time I was returning from the Maasland with my father in an empty cart hitched to a horse, and fell asleep. While I was asleep in the cart I must have tugged at the reins (or did I just dream that?), after which something dreadful occurred. But what? My father would no more say what it was than my mother could explain why we had been walking on that slope among the poppies as if we had been posing for Monet's painting *Wild Poppies*. Perhaps it seems so important because I do not know what happened. If I did know, it might turn out to be nothing in particular.

In my dream I saw my father walking among the poppies. I was standing on the dyke and saw him approaching. The sun was in his face and his shadow stretched out behind him as far as the village of Maasland. No matter how quickly he walked he failed to draw any closer. He saw me and waved, and his face was as I first remembered it as a boy: cheerful, with sparkling eyes, and that characteristic set of the mouth which made you laugh even before he did. His eyes shone in the sunlight and he hardly dragged the leg that had been maimed by a horse's kick. He wanted to tell me something or to call out something, for I heard him shout, "Mart, Mart..." but the rest was lost in the stillness around him and try as he might he drew no closer but remained at the same distance and I stood rooted to the spot, wanting to do something but paralysed and even unable to speak or wave. The oddest thing of all was that he was wearing bleached clogs — oh! how vividly that detail stood out — even though those bleached clogs should not have been visible at all in the thick grass among the poppies. And yet those clogs never stopped moving: he ran as though his life depended on it, even though he was anything but anxious or cast-down. No, he could scarcely have been in higher spirits.

It was a dreadful dream, mainly on account of that impotence, and the fact that it has become a little less dreadful over the years is only because it at least offers a chance of seeing him again as he once was when he used to cycle over the dyke with me in front.

That dream was the Binntal in the first few days. But the Binntal was also the pounding of stones, which reminded me so strongly of Ai van Leeuwen, the stonemason with whom my father had worked for so many years; and the Binntal was the Zumturm children, of whom I still did not know how many there were. The red heads of boys and girls stood out everywhere among the huts — a little girl still at the crawling stage, a boy already taller than his father. One almost had to walk as far the Italian border to escape them.

On a cloudless day we made an excursion to the Albrun pass. The sandy track led us deeper and deeper into the valley. Beyond a stream it narrowed to a footpath, winding its way among the rocks, sometimes getting lost in soggy ground and then turning up again later or, if it was not visible, indicated by a yellow mark on a rock. Gradually it became harder to find the path as it became increasingly covered in snow. But we pressed on doggedly, trudging along the broad Binna river valley, past the Albrunhütte and up to the pass. Here we were quite alone; the whole area was covered in fresh, white snow, the trail of footprints behind us standing out as grey, dark patches. We saw the border-stone well before we reached it. It led us upwards, but failed to explain why a set of footprints, that could also be traced down into the depths, should suddenly arise in the snow even though they did not follow the only possible route past the Hütte. Who on earth could have been wandering alone through the valley, such a short time ago? A frontier guard? A hiker who had stayed overnight in the hut and who had made a detour to the Italian border? We walked uneasily along the trail of footprints, which led up to the borderstone. When we got there the footprints abruptly stopped, as though the owner of those not particularly large mountain boots which had left such regular imprints in the snow had ascended into space from the border-stone. There were no footprints going back; nor were there any footprints to be seen further on. It was baffling — now there was a trail, and now it no longer existed, and one could hardly be expected to believe that the man or woman who had walked there had gone backwards placing his or her feet in exactly the same spots. The man or woman had, however, urinated near the stone — which tended to suggest it was man. In one spot the snow had melted and a small patch of dark earth was surrounded by a yellow border.

We stood there and the baffling trail marred our pleasure at having reached the border. We looked at the unrelenting emptiness of Italy — nothing but dark, black mountains and a wild valley without a trace of habitation and I looked once more at the trail of footprints and all at once I seemed again to be walking across that so rarely frequented quay behind the Maassluis town hall on New Year's Eve in 1962.

7

The heavenly emporium

On that New Year's Eve, at around ten o'clock, I walked through the deserted streets of Maasluis. Even the people who usually let off fireworks were missing on this evening because it was bitterly cold and had been snowing the whole evening. After it had stopped snowing I had gone straight away for a walk through the familiar streets. I had not been living in the town since the beginning of October but had been staying with my uncle and aunt in Leiden, and the pain this caused was just as acute as it had been three months earlier. It was not that I was badly treated by my uncle and aunt — on the contrary; but I longed for the familiar town and for my father's stories, which I now only heard at weekends, or did not hear at all, as I could not know what stories he had been telling during the week while I was in Leiden. And if I did hear one, it was often already beyond the first stage. For that was the best thing about them: the way in which those stories grew and changed, how they gradually became more colourful and adorned with untruths, which nevertheless helped bring out the atmosphere of the story. And I could no longer make a contribution myself. I would often say: "Was it really a third-class grave? It sounds more like a second-class grave to me, the way you're telling it." And then my father would say: "No, don't be silly, of course it was a third-class grave." But when I heard him tell the story again a few weeks later he would often have changed the detail, evidently realizing either consciously or unconsciously that the story was improved by working in the higher level of the second class. In this way I had often made minor contributions to his stories, which had become more and more animated — not, I should add, because of me but mainly because of my father's imagination — until the point was reached when the story was perfected and nothing more was changed. Sometimes his listeners would express doubts, but then my father would always say: "If it hasn't happened yet it still could," which left little room for argument.

During the weekend I asked endless questions — about the crew of the Volharding, about Ai van Leeuwen, about the undertakers, about the man who tended the little plot in front of his mother's grave so devotedly every day and cultivated the loveliest little plants, about the florists, about Quaavers who always solemnly addressed my father as "Paul" no matter how often my father protested that his name was Pau. Oh, it seemed as if I no longer had any part in those wonderful happenings at the cemetery: for that was it, that was life — that was quite another thing from drawing dead animals every afternoon in practical work, something I was punished with because I had refused to draw as a boy, even at secondary school, where the desperate art teacher had resorted to making me read out loud during the lesson. Yes, now that the cemetery and my father were so far away, it was as though, there in Leiden, I were not alive. And worst of all, there was not even a harbour in Leiden where I could walk. But then, if I were to stop studying and return to Maassluis I would have to enter national service, in which case I would once again be away from home: so there was no alternative to studying. And even in Leiden it could be very beautiful. I remembered clearly how there had been such a heavy mist over the city on the fifth of December that the houses and buildings could not be seen. Then, for the first time, I had walked contentedly through the streets, until I realized that I had been wondering for some time: *what is it that's missing?* The mournful, owl-like hooting of fog-horns on the river. There was a frost that night, and on the sixth the sun had revealed a world of magical beauty. Never before had I seen such magnificent hoar-frost on the trees or such white alder-cones sparkling in the sun and my uncle, who painted and liked to make use of slides, had taken enough pictures to last him for snow-scenes until the year two thousand — for those were his speciality, apart from still-lifes — and I had maintained stolidly to myself that it didn't matter a damn where I saw such hoar-frost on trees. But if my thoughts then turned to the little lane covered in hoar-frost in the cemetery near the gravediggers' shed, I would clench my fists in anguish.

But now I was walking in Maassluis again and my feet automatically headed for the quayside. Since I was fifteen I had developed the habit of walking through the harbour every evening. There would always be groups of girls walking about on the quayside who looked round at you half-laughing and who held out the prospect of an adventure beginning on the quay and ending among the goosefoot and dock on the banks of the Meuse. It did indeed begin that way for many boys and girls ending, after an intermezzo on the banks of the river, in or next to the child-bed; but I was too shamefaced even to approach a girl. I would just walk there, always longing anew for something that never happened, while other boys managed effortlessly to detach a girl from a group and to head off together to the Schanshoofd. Once, however, I nearly succeeded. I was walking along behind two girls and one of them had kept on looking round over her shoulder.

She giggled softly and I heard her say: "Would you dare to go to the river with him — not me!"

"She's a hot sort," said a boy I'd never seen before who suddenly emerged from the Zandpad and began walking next to me. "You take one and I'll take the other."

He caught up with them and began walking on the left beside the girl who had not been looking round, and I had little choice but to walk on the right next to the other girl. The boy casually put his arm around the girl's waist and I wanted to lift my arm up too but I could not; my arm felt heavier than a gravestone and as I just kept walking I heard the girl say: "What a creep," and yet she was still smiling and making eyes at me. It was her look, above all, which made me feel utterly despondent and which made me suddenly dash off. I could hear them calling after me: "Feeble prick!" before I disappeared around the corner of Fenacolius Street.

From that time onwards I had always wandered about the harbour later in the evening when the couples who had paired off would already be trampling on the sea-asters by the Meuse, for through those forays in quest of instant love I had become attached to the bluish shop-window lights, the smell of flour and tar oil and the sight of the illuminated red hands of the clock-tower; and above all to the melancholy, slightly salt atmosphere which, when you walked there all alone, made you feel you would live for ever.

But on that New Year's Eve I felt the urge to vary my route. Near the town hall I descended to the little quay behind the houses, which was only open to pedestrians. Why did I do that? I did not know, and only knew it had something to do with what my father had related at the dinner table in such a way that I was convinced he was not making things up or embroidering the truth.

"Just as I wanted to knock off at the end of the afternoon, this old fellow comes into the cemetery who I didn't know and had never seen before, with a large cap on so that I could hardly see his head and a dark scarf in front of his mouth, maybe because of the cold, maybe to show as little as possible of his pan, wearing black serge trousers and a long black coat, and says to me: 'Undertaker, I would....' 'I'm not an undertaker, even though I do undertake things,' I say to him. 'Sir,' he says, 'sooner or later we all become undertakers; the moment comes in everyone's lives that they have to bear the bad tidings to a relative: your father, your brother, your sister, your mother has died. You should remember that, sir. Have you never done anything like that?' 'Yes,' I say, 'when the old man died I had to tell all my brothers, because it happened to be my turn to watch over him when he suddenly wanted to go to the toilet in the night and tried to get up out of bed and fell dead in my arms. But by profession I'm not an undertaker's man, nor am I a foreman or a gardener or a stonemason; I'm a gravedigger here.' And he says: 'All right, gravedigger then, I'd like to ask you something strange.' 'If it's not stranger than my reply, go ahead,' I say. 'Well, it is rather odd,' he says, 'but I suppose you come across some odd things in your profession.' 'Yes, more than my father did in the cheese trade,' I say. 'Gravedigger,' he says from behind his scarf, which he warily held in place with his black mitten, 'gravedigger, I'm weary of life. I want to put an end to it tonight; I don't want to see in the New Year. Now if I put a stop to it tonight, where would I come to rest?' 'Are you from these parts? I've never seen you before.' 'I've just moved here,' he says, 'but I'll certainly be buried here. The question is: where?' 'Well,' I say, 'that depends on what you want. You can choose between a first-class private grave, second-class private grave or rented grave, third-class rented grave or fourth-class rented grave. But nowadays people no longer get buried in fourth-class graves. And if you're flat-broke you can also have a pauper's grave. The first class is pricey — three hundred guilders if not more; the third class costs you seventy-five guilders and then you get cleared out after twenty-nine years. But now you mention the subject,' I say, 'would you please put it off for as long as possible. It's been freezing since the twenty-second and there's three inches of frost in the ground — I can't even get a pick in. Yes, you'd be doing a great favour if you'd wait a bit.' 'But I badly wanted to put an end to things tonight,' he says. 'I really don't want to see in the New Year.' 'Don't be silly,' I say. 'You've kept going for quite a few years now and can surely wait a little longer. Once it stops freezing for a few days the frost will be out of the ground in no time.' 'But surely you've got other people to bury — you can't just stop digging.' 'Yes,' I say, 'but the more that come the more I've got to dig. I've still got two holes in the third class but there are already two waiting for them who'll be coming on the third of January, and after that I hope there'll be a bit of a gap. If you do yourself in tonight I'll have to start hacking away first thing in the New Year and that'll take me an entire morning because the ground is as hard as nails. Just a moment, come along to the third-class — I'll give you a pick and you can try for yourself.' So I walk with him in the darkness to the gravediggers' shed, fetch my pick and we walk to the third class where he tries to drive it into the ground. You should have seen his face! The pick wouldn't go in at all. 'Yes,' he says, 'I see what you mean. It might be better to wait a while after all.' 'Be a pal,' I say, 'and wait until the frost's gone. Then you can come back and I'll show you exactly where you'll come to rest. We can even arrange things very nicely between us — I'm not a bad chap, really — and you can more or less choose where you want to lie. Just come along and I'll show you where I'll be sticking in the next bodies and if you don't like the spot you can wait a bit and then once it does suit you, you string yourself up. You can even decide whether you want to lie on top, in the middle or underneath, whatever suits you best — everything can be arranged. But just wait until the ground's no longer frozen.' 'All right,' he says, 'I'll come again as soon as it stops freezing.' 'You do that,' I say, 'but remember that the ground can often stay frozen for a long time after the frost has gone.'"

What made me imagine that I would meet that man precisely there, on that out-of-the-way quay? And why did I believe that I might be able to persuade him differently? Perhaps my father had done just the right thing in asking him so matter-of-factly to hold off. No discussion of motives, no attempt to talk the man round — even though that might have been the real reason for his visit — but simply urging postponement, which could easily lead to abandonment. And yet it seemed as though my father had been remiss and that he should at least have said something about the undesirability of such an act. Or was it not undesirable? I would never have thought of suicide as a solution for irremediable homesickness as I bent over the drawing-paper, but the story had stimulated an idea, while at the same time offering an escape clause: I could not do so now in any case because the ground was frozen so far down.

No, the man was not there behind the town hall. There was nothing but virgin snow and I walked carefully along beside the houses.

Extraordinary, a man like that who came to ask where he would be buried if he were to commit suicide that evening. Perhaps he would do so after all, despite the frost.

I came across a set of footprints coming from the opposite direction. They curved away from the houses towards the water and I followed them. They must have been quite fresh because it had stopped snowing no more than ten minutes before. They led straight to the water's edge, and all I found at the brick edge of the quay was a firm imprint. There was no sign to be seen of there having been any dallying or standing about. The man or woman — although it must have been a man, because the footprints were even larger than mine — must have walked straight on. He had not paused or even taken a few extra steps, assuming he had boarded a boat. Admittedly it was conceivable that he had stepped straight from the quay on to a boat at much the same level. But in that case there would be signs in the snow at the edge of the quay, and I could see none. Even if the boat had been moored slightly away from the quay the man's final footsteps would have been different from the existing ones. No, the snow was perfectly intact, and the most likely thing was that the man had simply walked into the water.

I lent cautiously over the edge and peered into the oily water, which gleamed dully. I saw nothing to indicate the presence of a drowned person; silence lay over everything. Even the usual seagulls were missing. I could not shake off the notion that the footprints must belong to the man who had visited my father at the cemetery that afternoon. But that was impossible, and too absurd; the man had promised he would not. If he had done so, what was there to stop me from following his example? I was no longer able to stay at home day after day. The choice was between going to Leiden and doing something that made me feel almost ill — drawing — and military service. At home I had been forced to relinquish my garret with its hardboard panelling to my sister, and I now slept in a stuffy hole near the stairs. At my aunt's I had only a tiny, unheated room. It seemed I no longer belonged anywhere and as if there never would be a spot where I could feel at all happy again.

The bells of the Great Church disturbed my reverie, verging as it did so dangerously close to self-pity. What a bore I had become! Yes — a bore, that was what I was. The windows of the Great Church were illuminated and I felt as though I could hear the organ. But the footprints remained a disquieting mystery and I hurried away from the edge of the quayside rather more quickly than was prudent, since I could so easily have slipped over in the snow. It was as though I had gazed into an abyss: an abyss within me of which I had previously been totally unaware. As I drew closer to the steps leading to the dyke my courage returned, and the thought even occurred to me: of course, you've never had a girl-friend; the girls in Leiden all think you're too inoffensive to want to get to know you better, and yet somewhere in the world there's a girl meant for you. *But,* I thought, *right now she'll be celebrating New Year's Eve at home, eating the traditional Dutch doughnuts, and would be completely at a loss to understand that I like nothing more than to walk along a quayside all by myself.* "It's far better to stay alone," I mumbled firmly as I ascended the steps, leaving those uncanny footprints behind me. And so as to check my fear even further, I recited in time with my rising footsteps a poem I had read the week before in the university library reading room, and which had made such an impression on me that I had learned it by heart straight away:

Elysium is as far as to
The very nearest Room
If in that Room a Friend await
Felicity or Doom —

What fortitude the Soul contains,
That it can so endure
The accent of a coming Foot —
The opening of a Door —

And so I pulled myself together and the days slipped past, and it kept on freezing long after I was back in my aunt's little room, my legs wrapped in blankets and with all sorts of pullovers on by way of penance for the fact that I did not want to sit downstairs by the warm stove in the cosy sitting-room, where the blue light of the television flickered continuously.

I did not suffer from the cold, because with each day of frost the ground became a little deeper frozen, thus preventing the suicide of the man, whom I imagined to be very old. Every day it was freezing brought fresh hope; each night the temperature fell below freezing-point was another round won in the struggle against death. Why I should set so much store by the man's staying alive I could not understand, but each weekend I would anxiously ask my father whether the man had been back again yet. No, was the invariable reply. Nor had a drowned body been found in the new year; it was conceivable that the footprints could be accounted for by some other hypothesis than suicide, but it was also possible that the drowned person would only be washed up much later. However it turned out, there always remained hope as long as nobody had been found, and it kept on freezing as though it would never stop. Elephants in an English zoo were given rum to prevent them from being overcome by the cold; deer emerged from the woods begging for food; and as I cycled from Leiden to Maassluis, wearing two pairs of socks with a plastic bag in between and two caps and a pair of fur-lined gloves, I saw unfamiliar birds in the ice-holes in the Rhine-Schie canal. Beyond Delft I saw a goshawk perched on a pole, dying. One February afternoon, when dusk was already falling, a flock of twites came down from the icy sky into my uncle's garden and hopped into the unlocked aviary, the canaries all being in the living room. They remained where they were perfectly calmly, no matter how close we came. Fed by us they over-wintered in voluntary confinement, joined at first by two greenfinches and later even by a pair of bullfinches.

For me the frost meant no more than a stay of execution, but day after day my father sat gloomily by the red glow of the pot-bellied stove in the shed. There was very little he could do, besides which few people were dying because of the frost. "At last I've got this terrific sander," he said one weekend to a policeman who had recently been transferred to Maassluis and who had come to play draughts and was losing to him despite the fact that he had been draughts champion in the province of Gelderland. "For once the council lashes out and buys a sander and here I am holed up by this weather. I can't use it."

"Why not?" asked the policeman.

"Well, you see, water comes out of the machine as you sand. It's a neat idea but the water freezes as you work."

"What do you need water for anyway?"

"What do I need water for? What do you think I need the sander for?"

"No idea. Perhaps for sanding wood."

"Sanding wood? In a cemetery? Coffins, you mean? Don't be absurd! Anyway, you make sure you take a whitewood coffin, not an oak one and least of all a pine one — they rot so damned slowly. When the graves have to be cleared out you can suddenly strike a brand-new coffin, and then the body is usually intact as well. Then you're in a pretty fix. How do you get rid of the corpse?"

"Enough of your disgusting stories. You were going to tell me what you use that sander for."

"To clean gravestones."

"Do you clean all the gravestones?"

"No, only those down for maintenance. You can register a stone for maintenance with the council. It costs twenty guilders and I've got to keep it clean and to paint the lettering black again. For heaven's sake don't have a stone, will you? It's the worst thing there is for a gravedigger, if only because of the grass that has to be cut away from around the stones because you can't get at it with a motor-mower."

"So you need a sander to clean the stones?"

"Ah, at last the penny's dropped! You're a real copper, born thick and always thick. That's right, that's what I've got a sander for."

He paused for a moment to take three of his opponent's pieces with a gesture of the utmost dexterity. He continued:

"I used to do it all by hand, with a sanding block, and that worked fine; that's not the point. You'd clean one of those stones up perfectly and paint it and then relatives would come along to look — usually matrons, because women will pay to have their husband's stone maintained but men won't — only to find that two or three of those big wood-pigeons had shat on it. Time and again people would go and complain at the council offices. And they complained too that the lettering hadn't been painted nicely enough — not to me, they wouldn't dare, because I'd abuse those women to within an inch of their lives, but to the man at the counter. And then of course along comes Quaavers on his high horse. Well, I only had to hear one such complaint and I'd try to sand the lettering right off the stone. That's no problem where the letters are raised; you can just sand them off. But it's quite impossible with stones where the lettering has been cut in. Then you've got to sand the whole stone down and that's one hell of a job. But with the machine it's fantastic: in an hour you can get the stone completely smooth so there's not a letter to be seen. They come up splendidly, all clean and bright, and I can tell you that any stone they complain about gets sanded down as flat and free of letters as this draughts-board. Pity it's so cold now, because I've got quite a few stones earmarked for treatment. Yes, and then they come along and ask: 'Gardener —' that's what one of them called me just the other day — 'gardener, I can't read my grandfather's name any more.' 'Yes, madam, that stone's down for maintenance with an asterisk. That means there were complaints last time that it wasn't properly cleaned, so this time I gave it extra special treatment. Yes, pity about the lettering — it was so far gone I couldn't even paint it any more.' 'How dreadful,' the matron said. 'Why?' I asked. 'Can't you remember what the words said?' 'Yes,' she said. 'Here it said "Rest in Peace" and my grandpa's name was here and then there it said: "A dear name glides in the clouds." ' 'And don't you know your grandfather's name any more then?' 'Yes, of course,' she said. 'Well, then,' I said, 'why should his name and Rest in Peace and that verse be on the stone? You know it all anyway.' 'For other people,' she said, 'To read.' 'Oh,' I said, 'do you think that other people bother to read what's written on stones where totally unknown people are buried? Putting something on a gravestone is of no use to anyone — close relatives know anyway and others aren't interested.' "

Once again he took a couple of the policeman's pieces, whose face reddened as he saw defeat looming up.

"There's no greater bugbear than painting the lettering on a gravestone," my father said, "and if on top of that they start complaining, well, they'll know all about it. If it was up to me there would be a law against gravestones as from half-past seven tomorrow morning. They're nothing but a confounded nuisance, first of all when graves are cleared out and you have to get one of those thumping great weights off, and secondly when mowing the grass...."

"Yes, you said that before," the policeman said irritably.

"Thirdly, if one of those stones is down for maintenance and the birds shit all over it when it's just been painted. I enjoy my work and wouldn't swap it for anything else except for a small mixed farm with ten cows, some arable land and a nice bit of meadow, but gravestones are my pet hate. Well, that was it. Can't they play draughts in Gelderland? Like another game?"

He set up the pieces again.

"I heard," he said to the policeman, "that your wife is keen on literature. My son here is too. I'm not. We always used to read the same books. I read his boys' books and his detective stories as he got a bit older, but then one day he brought home *Karakter* by Bordewijk. Do you know the book?"

"No, never heard of it," said the policeman.

"Well, you're not missing anything. It's about a father who virtually helps his son into the grave. And that was meant to be literature. Since then we have parted ways on that score. It's a pity, we used to read the same books; but I can do without literature, especially that book by Bordewijk. That rotten father treating his son like a beast, a real bastard he was."

All at once he turned to me with a totally different question. "Couldn't you ask my brother-in-law if he's got a speech for me? It's my turn again at the men's meeting and he always has such fine subjects."

The next day, when I had returned to Leiden, I asked my uncle for a speech.

"The best thing I've got," said my uncle, "is a speech about the problem of where Jesus got his clothes from when he rose from the dead on the third day. You'll remember he was buried naked but did not reappear naked."

"Where did those clothes come from then?" I asked.

"From the heavenly emporium," my uncle said solemnly. "I quoted the Scriptures in support. It's a splendid subject and your father's free to borrow it, but tell him to use it sparingly."

And so the next weekend I brought along an exercise book containing a talk on the heavenly emporium, and since my father did not wish it to be apparent at the men's meeting "Faith and Scripture" that he had got the talk from someone else, he learned it off by heart sentence by sentence. That took him three weeks, sometimes in the front room of our house but usually beside his pot-bellied stove in the gravediggers' shed because there was nothing he could do outside anyway. Since he always liked to bellow at the top of his voice when learning a text off by heart I would have loved to have seen how visitors to the cemetery reacted to the strange sounds coming from the shed. But I was unable to skulk around the cemetery because I had to extract dead animals from alcohol and to copy skeletons as though I were Tom Traddles.

My father was far from satisfied with his brother-in-law's text. One Sunday in February he was having his afternoon nap on two chairs in the sitting-room. From outside there came the sound of a passing ship's horn, and in his sleep my father responded to the call with an astonishingly clever imitation of the sound. A moment later he woke up, sat up straight and, looking at me, said: "It's not true at all."

"What's not true?" I asked.

"About those clothes. Those clothes didn't come from the heavenly emporium at all. What does the Bible say about Mary Magdalene when she sees Jesus?"

"She thought he was the gardener," I said.

"Exactly, that's what it says. And what do they sometimes say to me? They say: 'Gardener, can you tell me where I can find my mother's grave?' Mary Magdalene thought she had seen the gravedigger, which is not really so surprising because she was walking through a cemetery. Do you know what happened? Jesus rose from the tomb, went over to the gravedigger's shed and put on the gravedigger's clothes. It was not beneath his dignity to look as I do. Do you think he might have worn clogs as well? In any case: not the heavenly emporium."

"What are you going to do now?"

"I know it by heart now. If I alter it they won't listen to me anyway. You know what Acts 27:11 says: 'Nevertheless they believed the master and the owner of the ship, more than those things which were spoken by Paul.'"

It kept on freezing. On weekends I saw ice-floes in the harbour. Even the sea froze over. My father was only able to dig a grave when assisted by all the road-makers and council gardeners who had been put out of work by the cold weather. Sometimes they would hack away for an entire day at the same small patch of ground, which was becoming deeper frozen night by night. The accounts I came to hear on Saturdays and Sundays were colourful but already embroidered with lies. Not that they were usually told to me, but to the Gelderland draughts champion. Intent on revenge he would turn up every Saturday evening and, being forced to stay in the sitting-room for want of a room of my own, I would hear all my father told him.

"Well, I'll be blessed if the strangest thing didn't happen to me this week," my father said to him. "One morning I wake up and go to get my dentures out of the glass of water next to my bed to put them in and what do you think happens? I can't get them out: frozen stuck in the glass. I can't do a thing at the cemetery without my dentures."

Oddly enough he did not explain why he so often needed his dentures at the cemetery. When desperate, he had the habit of getting rid of persistent, difficult visitors whom he could not persuade to leave in the normal way by speaking to them with his dentures half out of his mouth, so as to give them a foretaste of what they might expect once they were under the ground. Then he would jam his habitual cigarette between his false teeth, giving him an even more gruesome appearance. Of all his odd habits, this was perhaps the most distasteful, but I must admit it frequently proved a patent remedy against the sorts of men he began talking to the policeman about.

"The worst," he said, "are those odd fish who sometimes appear at the cemetery in the evening when it's dark. You never know where they've come from — they're always strangers — but you can tell what they're after just from the way they shuffle about."

"What are they after?" asked the policeman.

"I can't put it into ordinary language, the words don't exist; but with me they don't get a chance. After each burial I always make sure that the coffin is fully covered with sand so that they can't open it. It beats me completely — what possesses those blokes?"

"But why do they want to open up the coffins of people who have just been buried?"

"They want to open up women's coffins."

"But why?"

"Don't you understand?"

"Well, no, do they want to look at the body?"

"If only that was all it was."

"Do they want to rob it?"

"What can you steal from a corpse? A wedding ring? No, it's not that."

"You've got a fascinating profession," said the policeman.

They looked at each other for some time and eventually my father said: "I really don't think you get it. And you a draughts champion. Well, that doesn't count for a row of beans. I haven't lost a single game to you yet. Were you really Gelderland draughts champion?"

"I was junior champion of Gelderland while you were still in nappies."

"I don't doubt it. A junior draughts champion was brought into the cemetery just the other day, a boy who had killed himself on his moped. They put him in the mortuary, injured all over — you know, Isaiah 1.6 — and we were standing...."

"What does Isaiah 1.6 say?"

"Don't you know?" my father asked in astonishment.

"No, why should I know?"

"You're a Christian, aren't you?"

"Yes, I'm a Calvinist."

"Then you should know what Isaiah 1.6 says. It says: 'From the sole of the foot even unto the head there is no soundness in it; but wounds, and bruises, and putrefying sores: they have not been closed, neither bound up, neither mollified with ointment.' Strange you don't know that. So there we were talking about it a bit, the doctor, the police officer and the two ambulance men who had brought him in, and me, and then you should have heard that moped rider, junior champion of South Holland, belch! Gas build-up in the stomach; it happens sometimes. The doctor got such a fright I could almost have buried him on the spot but I said: 'Pass me a hammer and I'll finish the boy off.' Anyway, off they went and I stayed behind and mopped up some blood off the floor. While I'm crawling over the floor I suddenly get this terrific clout on the brainpan. Yes, I think he knew I would have beaten him at draughts, junior champion or not.''

From the way in which my father was telling the story you could discern that he had the upper hand in the game. I thought there would be more to come from the way he beamed at the board.

"And what do you think of that woman who came in the other day. She had heard that her husband's grave was to be cleared out. She asks: 'What do you expect to find, gardener?' I say: 'Bones, madam.' 'And what will you be doing with them?' she asks. 'I'll put them in a box,' I say. 'Yes, but how can you be sure that you've got all my husband's bones?' 'Madam,' I say, 'I can't guarantee that I'll put all the right bones together, but to do you a favour I'll stick in a few extra.'''

"A dreadful profession," said the brick-red policeman.

"Yes," said my father, "it's developed into a nice end-game. The worst thing, the very worst thing I ever...."

His lips began to tremble, the policeman looked up in surprise and my father said: "Sand on top."

Two tears slid down the cheeks towards the draughts-board. I knew what he had wanted to tell the policeman but had been unable to put into words: how on one occasion he had been forced to exhume the grave of his brother Henk who had come to grief in the rope factory. I was glad he did not tell the story but quickly returned to the subject of his dentures.

"I can hardly put it on a warmer all night," he said, "so I wrap a little blanket around the glass instead. What do you do with your dentures?"

"I haven't got false teeth," said the policeman.

"Haven't got false teeth? A man of your age? Still got your own teeth? How unlucky can you be! Endless toothache and misery — I really feel for you."

"I never get toothache."

"Impossible. Do you know another thing that can give you

trouble?"

"My teeth don't give me any trouble at all."

"No, I mean at the cemetery: there are always people who bring along their cat or dog. Attendant, would you please bury it for me? I do have a spot set aside but I shouldn't really do it."

And there was another thing I missed about those first two months of 1963. During the period it was freezing my father saw the most unusual birds in the cemetery, and because of this he was able to predict at the end of February that the winter would soon come to an end.

"All my birds have gone," he told me on the last weekend in February. "The frosts are over."

"Then that man might come back again," I said.

"Of course not," he said. "We'll never see him again."

And so in fact it seemed. For several days in March it had stopped freezing and the man had still not reappeared at the cemetery.

One Saturday afternoon I was standing on the Zuidvliet bridge, looking at the flowing water. The lock leading to the harbour had been opened because it was ebb-tide and the melt-water could be easily drained off since the water-level in the harbour was much lower than that in the channel. Small icefloes were drifting on the swiftly flowing water. But it was not that which made the swift stream below me so fascinating. Dead fish were drifting between the ice-floes. Drifting towards the sea I saw large carp and rudd and sprats and fat eel and enormous bream. Many of the fish were drifting with their stomachs uppermost so that all one saw was white and sometimes a patch of red on the ventral fins. I looked and looked; it just went on and on, with a strange, unvarying and inscrutable regularity: now more carp, now more roach or rudd with their still bright-red fins, and occasionally a white bream or an ide or the much darker tench. Sometimes I even thought I caught a glimpse of the barbels of a sheatfish, or a small school of bitterlings would pass by. But most shocking of all were the crucian carp, not because they were as dead as all the other fish, but because they were much bigger than I had ever seen before. This meant, I realized, that even these, the largest of them all, and which were usually never to be caught, had perished from lack of oxygen. Pike and perch also drifted by among the rudd, predator and prey reconciled in death. Every inch of the water flowing by was covered with dead fishes, which sometimes even pushed aside the ice-floes and which, neatly arranged by the current, were on their way to the harbour basin. I gazed at the sight with tears in my eyes, not because I was moved but because I kept forgetting to blink. No, it was not something to feel moved about; it was too gripping for pity and it also went on too long for that. The water flowed on and on as long as the tide continued to ebb, and all that time dead fish were going by. On Sunday the locks were opened again at ebb-tide and once more all sorts of dead rudd and bream and ide went by, as though they were on their way to sea once again, and yet they were different fish. It was something that transcended all sense and understanding: these enormous numbers, even just there, in the Zuidvliet and the waters in the polder reservoirs behind.

It was the sight of the dead fish which somehow convinced me that the man would return, and so it was: the week after the drainage of the melt-water with the dead fish he called on my father.

"Can I do it now?"

"By thunder, can't you wait! The ground's still frozen a yard and a half deep. It'll be nearly high summer before that's gone."

In this way my father managed to secure postponement but each week I would cycle home in anxious suspense: might it have happened? And every Saturday I would be told that the man had been and had been sent away. Because it was becoming springlike I was less troubled by my insistent feelings of homesickness; coltsfoot was springing up between the last patches of snow and the banks of ditches were coloured yellow by lesser celandine. I simply could not understand that that did not form sufficient reason for the man to want to stay alive. My father conducted lengthy conversations with him, referring to the "sole solace of both life and death" of the Heidelberg Catechism, but the man insisted that the Bible nowhere explicitly forbade suicide. My father of course referred to King Saul and to Judas, but the man maintained that the one had been condemned for disobedience and the other for betrayal. Their suicide itself was not condemned. And so the frost in the ground remained the sole hope and for a long time my father was able to maintain that the ground remained frozen deep and made grave-digging a torment. But one day my father was digging a grave, singing lustily about the girl who was given a ball and fell into the dark canal, and after he had been shovelling sand up effortlessly for an hour, he saw the man standing under a rhododendron shrub.

The man came up and said: "It's going well today."

"Once you get through that damned initial layer of frost," said my father.

"Well, I've been here from the moment you began; I thought I'd hide behind this big bush and I didn't see any sign of hacking. You've been singing cheerfully the whole time. If I do it now, I'll probably come to lie in that grave. Well, that would suit me fine. See you later, then."

My father told this on a Sunday evening and I can still see his hand hovering above the chess-board, stopping when it came to the queen.

"What I can't understand," he said, "is why he said see you later."

"Why not?" I asked.

"Because he hanged himself the same evening."

"But wasn't he laid out on a bier in the mortuary afterwards?"

"Yes, that.... Do you think that's why he said see you later?"

"I think so," I said.

But my father was not listening and simply said: "He needn't have taken it so literally."

"What?" I asked.

"That I said: once it stops freezing you can string yourself up. He could have used poison or gas instead, couldn't he?"

8

The helicopter

In the evening the house was eerily surrounded by dozens of bats which, like the Zumturms, varied greatly in size. All they needed was to have red hair as well: or perhaps they had but it was not visible in the darkness. For it was so dark at Imfeld at night that you could easily have printed photographs in the open air. Evening upon evening I stood in the minuscule village square, which my presence alone made seem over-crowded, especially if a little red-haired Zumturm should happen to be peeping round the corner of a hut. As the bats brushed past me and moths settled on my shoulders to avoid being caught by the bats, I looked at the stars and recalled how as a child I used to think that every star was the light of a dead person in heaven. No part of the sky was without stars, from which you could tell how full heaven already was. "There is no room for any more dead people," I said to myself in a desperate attempt to bring my father's illness to a halt. But at the same time the star-studded sky radiated such a sense of peace that not only could I "not get my fill" like Matthias Claudius, but the bitterness and rage directed towards everything and everyone, and especially against the elderly, grew less day by day and it began to seem that, if not at that moment then at least later, I would be able to accept that my father and by extension I myself would have to die. And each evening I was able to mumble Matthias Claudius's poem with greater conviction beneath the starry sky:

> At midnight, labours done,
> When all in bed do lie,
> I often gaze upon
> The vast and starry sky.

And when I went home to bed I could not help thinking of the end of the poem and that I was unable to recite it because a lump always came to my throat at the last words:

Beneath the canopy of heaven
My heart then said to me:
"This world has better things than all
Thy joys and misery."

I fling myself upon my bed
And lie awake for hours
And yearn to find out what was meant,
With all my mental powers.

But I lay awake not only because I longed for "better things" in "this world" but because I was afraid and listened to all the mysterious noises in and outside the house. I thought: *If only my father were here, how peacefully I would sleep.*

Because it could already get very cold at night, we lit a fire in the soapstone fireplace dating to 1601. Every other day I would fetch bread from the only shop in Binn, walking along a narrow mountain path high above the Binna, which was still so far from the sea that it felt it necessary to rush in that direction as fast as it could. I used to wonder whether a rock-collector would have taken the bread if I had left it on the path, because it was so hard that a mason's tools would have been more to the point than a knife.

We walked all over the valley and did not discuss the mysterious footprints any more. But one day we saw somebody walking with skis over his shoulder and this gave Hanneke the idea that the man might have proceeded on skis at the Italian border, and that this was why the footprints had ceased.

"But then we would have seen a ski-trail," I said. "Then again we weren't looking for one — we could easily have overlooked it."

Yes, that had to be the explanation to the mystery, but the limited sense of satisfaction I felt at that suggestion was set at nought by the fact that there was no comparable explanation for the trail of footprints on New Year's Eve. And why was it so important to me to clear the matter up?

And then in the Binntal, which — with the exception of the Binna itself — was so peaceful, there happened something that suggested a different explanation for the vanished footprints.

One evening after we had eaten we were sitting on the benches attached to the walls of the house and looked out over the valley. The sun was already low but still lit up the entire eastern face of the mountain-chain bordering one side of the valley. Above the dividing line between light and shade, which more or less followed the course of the Binna, there suddenly appeared a red speck which stood out clearly against the brown wall of the Breithorn. The speck seemed to be climbing higher against the mountain and yet at the same time to be growing larger. This was so paradoxical that I simply stared at the red monster without even pausing to wonder what it might be. The gradually growing speck emitted a noise out of all proportion to its size: a booming sound that reverberated a thousand-fold among the mountain walls, filling the valley with incessant, rumbling thunder. We were not the only ones to hear the sound and to see the speck; below the house Zumturms streamed past to the edge of the village. I even saw a very old Zumturm emerge from the house in which they all lived — a Zumturm I had never seen before, a great-great grandfather with such bowed legs that at each step he bumped his right knee on his walking-stick, which as it was he was holding at arm's length. His beard was snow-white, and of his undoubtedly once-red hair there remained no more than a half-inch wreath of pure white fluff beneath his head-gear.

Meanwhile the red speck was growing larger and still I did not know what it was. I could see that it was flying swiftly but why was it taking so long to cover the distance from the Breithorn to Imfeld? It was not until the speck flew over Binn that I saw it was a blood-red helicopter. Since people were flocking from all directions we too left the house to join in the general excitement. Preparations were being made for the helicopter to land in a large meadow near the turbulent, rushing Binna. A heavy rope had been stretched across the Binna and Hanneke conjectured that it might be some sort of exercise. That seemed likely to me too; there was the same sort of atmosphere as when the volunteer fire-brigade used to practise in Maassluis. My father particularly liked acting the part of victim in such exercises; dressed like a farmer, with a piglet under his arm, he would be dragged groaning loudly from a derelict farmhouse that had been set on fire.

The helicopter hovered above the paddock and a man in a diving-suit descended by a rope-ladder, and as he did so I could picture how the man who had left the footprints could have climbed up the rope-ladder after having reached the border. The diver went to the Binna and slipped into the water, holding firmly on to the rope with both hands. Even so he was instantly caught in the boiling foam and disappeared entirely for a moment, surfacing again immediately, his body having been swept through 180 degrees. He appeared to be dancing in the water and he returned to the bank straight away. Even that caused him difficulty, despite the fact that he had danced no more than a half yard towards the centre of the Binna. One of the Zumturms knotted a stout rope around his waist and the diver entered the water again, this time with three Zumturms holding on to the rope. I looked at the spectators; everywhere red Zumturm hair was lit up in the rays of the setting sun. I began counting resolutely: at last I would be able to find out how many there were. But since they kept on moving and the little ones had begun playing some sort of tag, I had to keep on starting with the great-great grandfather again, one, and then the mother, two, and then the three Zumturms on the rope, three, four and five, but from then on it became difficult. Apart from anything else the giant blades of the helicopter were turning round so swiftly in order to keep it ten feet off the ground that a storm-wind tore across the field, making everyone scurry for cover. I soon stopped counting; nor was I to know now how many Zumturms there were in all. In any case, three of them were still standing on the bank of the Binna, holding on to the rope fastened to the diver struggling desperately in the raging foam.

"Do you think he's meant to cross the river on the rope?" I asked Hanneke.

"Perhaps the idea is just to reach that clump of rock in the middle," she said.

That seemed indeed to be the case. But there was no question of the diver even getting within a yard of it. At a certain point it was evident from the way in which the Zumturms were taking in the slack rather than letting the rope out that the diver had turned back, but he might just as well have been on his way to the boulder. Sometimes he even disappeared beneath the water for such a long time that you feared he would never surface again. The helicopter blades began turning more rapidly, the trees beside the Binna were almost pressed flat to the ground, and the helicopter ascended and suddenly flew off towards Binn. Then, in the deep-yellow sunlight, it veered and in a perfectly executed slalom approached over the water, simply buffeting lots of the onlookers to the ground. The trees by the Binna were compressed into small bushes, so that the rushing water became more clearly visible. The helicopter remained suspended directly over the Binna and I looked at the sun spinning round in the sparkling silver blades. The struggling diver caught in the foaming water reached the bank and was dragged ashore exhausted. A second diver descended from the helicopter by means of the rope-ladder and disappeared into the water near the boulder, where he seemed able to stand and even to lean against the granite. Only his dark head still appeared above the water and now and then you could see his black hands doing something in the foam that seemed to require a good deal of strength. I was still standing on the sandy track running past the meadow but Hanneke had managed to find a sheltered spot on the other side of the field near the Binna.

The man in the foam raised one of his arms and the helicopter rose vertically, pulling him out of the water as it went. His black diving-suit glistened as the water ran off. There might almost have been a magical beauty about that glistening blackness covered in drops of water sparkling in the sunlight if a second body had not been drawn out of the water below the man on the rope, with the same, uniform motion. I only looked at it for an instant before turning away, for it was one of those images you feel you have dreamed a hundred times, an image you know, in the single, split second in which it appears on the retina, will remain indelibly etched on the mind. The youth — for it was a youth who was hanging below the diver's black feet — had blond hair and his head hung forward, with his arms hanging limply past his head, and those arms were still partly uncovered by an unbuttoned, trailing blue shirt that was heavy with water, as were the white trousers clinging to his legs. Above all it was the strange, smooth arch of the body, hanging down from the waist on both sides in a way that otherwise only trained ballet dancers can achieve, that left one in absolutely no doubt: *the boy is dead.* I walked away as the helicopter descended again and let the boy down on the meadow, in between where Hanneke and I were standing. She stayed where she was while all the other onlookers raced towards the dead boy with a sort of eagerness and haste which, combined with the storm-wind, made many of them stumble. They formed a thick hedge around the boy, who was no longer to be seen. I felt amazed at the way all those onlookers had run; I too wanted to run, but as far away as possible from the drowned person in the grass.

As I climbed towards Imfeld and Hanneke quickly followed me, the red helicopter flew off at breathtaking speed, much more quickly than it had come. One moment it still filled the sky, the next it was a speck near the Breithorn becoming smaller during its apparent descent and suddenly dissolving like a wisp of red steam in the evening sun.

When we had returned to the house and were looking at the still considerable activity on the meadow near the river and at the arrival of an ambulance, the little girl returned who had shown us the wrong house on our first day in the Binntal. Right below our house, on the corner of the path in the open patch between the man-sized thistles, she met another little Zumturm, a younger sister, who had apparently seen nothing of what had happened. They stood there in the setting sun while the little girl listened and her sister, who had the finest red hair of all the Zumturms, told her slowly and solemnly what had happened. She illustrated her account with all sorts of poses and positions of her body. Now you could see the diver going under the water, now he emerged again. Then the rope was paid out by her brothers, then it was hauled in again. At the end of her tale she suddenly bent over backwards and let her arms hang loosely, while on her face there appeared something which could only be termed horror. For some time she remained motionlessly in the same attitude, possibly not only so as to show her sister how the boy had been slumped as he was hauled up, but also to come to terms with the image herself. She was only little — too little really to curve her body sufficiently, although it helped that she had so much red hair that could hang free. The other girl tried to copy her — and actually managed, even though she was even smaller. They stood up straight again, bent over once more, stood up again, and let their hands and heads flop backwards again. If I had not known anything I would have thought they were playing a game or practising some exercises, and I might even have laughed at the droll movements of those two little girls with their red hair. The girls suddenly laughed too; they shrieked with laughter and, bending and swaying, made their way between the huts to the large house belonging to the Zumturm family. Their laughter died away among all the rickety buildings and when they had gone an unreal silence fell. In particular there was one sound I missed and I tried to pinpoint it. I shut my eyes and suddenly I knew: even at that hour of the day one usually heard the sound of the last stone-breakers in search of minerals. Now I could not hear them, presumably because they were all at the Binna looking at the dead boy.

What had been the sound of that noise — was it really the same sound as that in Ai van Leeuwen's stonemason's yard? As I tried to recall the sound by means of that detour I saw Ai van Leeuwen himself before me, and I saw a prostrate stone that he and my father were trying vainly to budge.

9

The exhumation

I had asked him at least a dozen times and each time he had said: "No."

"But why not?"

"Because you're still far too young. And it's not allowed; nobody's allowed in the cemetery when a grave's exhumed."

But no matter how often he said that I was not convinced. I thought it so strange that it should not be possible. I had been to the market with my father; it was from him that I had learned in the garden the garden in the Westgaag how lettuce was planted and how to thin out grapes and load up a truck. Why could I not join in now? I was after all allowed to see how my father dug a grave, how he mowed the plots, sanded back the stones and then painted in the words, how he drew lines over the paths between the plots on Saturday mornings and raked up the leaves in autumn. But this was not permitted. There was only one comfort: nobody was allowed to be present. But that one Wednesday afternoon I was deprived of this comfort, for my father told my grandmother, who was visiting us: "Exhumation this afternoon."

Nobody replied, because there was something threatening about the word, something different from everything else associated with burials or sanding stones or mowing grass or raking leaves.

"It's going to be quite a job," said my father. "First of all a slab on the ground has to be moved."

"Surely you can't manage that all by yourself?" asked my grandmother.

"No, Ai van Leeuwen the stonemason is going to help me."

I suddenly stared my father straight in the face.

"And you always said," I said indignantly, "that nobody was allowed to be present at an exhumation."

"Yes, but I can't remove that stone by myself. I need a skilled labourer."

"He's allowed to be present but I'm not," I said, panting with rage.

It was little less than treason. I shoved my plate away and began sobbing uncontrollably. We did everything together and now I was not allowed to come along and Ai van Leeuwen the stonemason was allowed to be present.

"I'll give you a thick ear," said my father. "Then at least you'll have something to cry about."

However, I had heard that threat so often that I didn't shed a single tear less and when he did in fact hit me, because he could not stand people crying, I only bent forward even more and sobbed: "He can and I can't, he can and I can't."

"Couldn't he go just once?" my grandmother asked.

"You know it's not allowed. You can't bring a child along when a grave's being dug up."

"How old is this grave?"

"Ninety-nine years on the dot — it's a first-class grave, you see; the longest you stay in the third class is thirty years."

"As long as that? In that case there'll be nothing left, just a few bones. That wouldn't be too bad, would it?"

"Perhaps not, but I don't like the idea."

"It wouldn't be the first time he had seen bones, would it?"

"Yes," I said, "at the butcher's — I'm not really scared and would love to come."

"Well, all right then," said my father. "As long as you keep out of the way."

But it did not prove so easy to attend an exhumation, for when we reached the cemetery Ai van Leeuwen was standing there in a pair of dirty blue overalls, waiting with a large crowbar and a jack.

"What's the kid doing here?" he asked.

"He badly wanted to come along for once."

"Impossible. A child at an exhumation — you must be out of your mind."

"That feller's been there for ninety-nine years. There's nothing left."

"Are you sure? And what if it's mummified? A fine pickle we'd be in then with a child around."

"Then I'd tell him to clear off — he'd have to go to the shed."

"He'll have to go once we've removed the stone."

How wonderfully exciting that exchange was! It meant that something very special was going to happen, something that I had not only never experienced but that belonged to the world of grown-ups. The sun itself seemed to shine more brightly as we walked along the paths, me following my father to one side, he, with a strange force, dragging his leg that had been lamed by a mare. I was carrying a small crowbar, which gave me a feeling not only of being involved but of being indispensable. I looked up past Ai van Leeuwen's tall shoulder towards the scudding white clouds whose shadows were continually gliding over the paths, plots and gravestones. The small trees near the gravestones rustled in the breeze and the air was filled with the cooing of wood-pigeons. We reached the stone. I stood still and looked at the hedge behind. A hedge-sparrow took no notice of us but kept steadily building its barely visible nest. My father fetched a wheelbarrow and I looked at the gravestone. It was a slate-coloured slab on a bit of a slope; it looked as though he were resting on a pillow. The letters of his name were as illegible as the dates below. But at the bottom of the stone was a rhymed couplet:

You who gaze upon these stones
Like me will turn to dust and bones.

"Not me," I said out loud when I had read the rhyme.

"What do you mean, not me?" asked Ai van Leeuwen.

"Well, that we'll become like that too."

"I rather think we will."

"It's not true! The Lord Jesus will be coming back on a heavenly cloud and then we'll all be going to meet the Lord on a cloud, safe and sound."

"What makes you so sure?"

"The minister said so on Sunday."

"Maybe; ministers say all sorts of things — that's what they're paid for."

"He's coming back. The moon just had a halo."

"Well, let's hope so and preferably straight away, because how on earth are we going to move this brute?"

He stared at the gravestone and I looked at the scudding clouds. Perhaps they were angels who would come down at any moment. They would push aside the stones with their wings and people would rise up from their graves.

But when my father returned with the wheelbarrow, ropes, some more crowbars and all sorts of other equipment, there commenced a long struggle with the slab. For half an hour, no matter how they strained and heaved, it refused to budge but lay there with a strange sort of immovability, defying not just the swift clouds whose shadows brushed over the stone so playfully but also the sweat worked up by my father and Ai van Leeuwen, which they wiped away from time to time with a quick lift of the cap or hat.

"We'll never shift this brute," Ai van Leeuwen panted.

"We might if you kept your great clodhoppers off the stone every time I stick in the crowbar," my father said.

"Yes, thanks very much, if it starts to slip and lands on my foot I'll be stuck here for good."

"One of these days you'll end up here anyway."

"But without mangled feet if you don't mind."

"Would you just mind sticking your crowbar in a bit more to the left. You tackle things in such a ham-fisted way — I suppose you're from the Westland, are you?"

"Well, what of it?"

"The wise men came from the east."

"And when they had been the Bethlehem stonemason had quite a few gravestones to make for children."

"If he was one of your sort he must have made a mint."

The stone moved for the first time, by no more than an inch.

"Hurrah!" Ai van Leeuwen shouted. He threw his indescribably dirty, dark-brown hat in the air, where it was caught in a gust of wind and carried off to a neighbouring plot as yet uncovered by stones, where it bounded and capered across the grass in front of his outstretched hands, coming to rest, after the wind had lifted it up once more, on a simple wooden cross marking a grave. He retrieved the hat primly and placed it on his enormous skull.

"Well, that's a start," he said.

"All's not well that starts well," said my father.

For the moment, no matter how they toiled, that was as far as they got, while from the opposite side of the railway which ran past the cemetery, snatches of sound were carried in the gusting wind. At Key & Kramer huge cranes wafted long pipes through the air like feathers, even though they were far heavier than that implacable gravestone. The hedge-sparrow kept on bringing straws to its nest while a blackbird bustled about unconcernedly among the stones right next to us. Birds are much tamer at a cemetery than elsewhere; they have nothing to fear from the dead.

Just as the stone began to show signs of moving we were startled by a loud shout. Looking up we saw a man behind the cemetery fence. He struck the wire-netting with both fists and shouted: "You're not getting me yet!"

"That's Kees Vreugdenhil," my father said.

Ai van Leeuwen lifted up his hat and cupped his hand behind his ear.

"What's he yelling?"

"'You're not getting me yet,'" said my father. "He's been saying that for a couple of years now. He comes by every day to let us know."

"Yes," I said proudly, "I've seen him lots of times too."

"Go on with you," said Ai van Leeuwen.

"Don't you believe me? You can see for yourself, can't you?"

My father cupped his hands to his mouth.

"Come here if you dare," he called out.

"You're not getting me yet!" the man shouted back.

"He used to come into the cemetery to tell me I wouldn't be getting him yet. He'd creep up on me over the grass; usually I would see him but sometimes I didn't," my father explained. "I'd be sanding back a stone or digging a grave and then he'd suddenly shout in my ear: 'You're not getting me yet!' I got heartily sick of it and nearly jumped out of my skin each time. One time he had crept up on me again behind the stones, and I came up out of a grave where I had just hammered in the last plank and I saw him before he could say a thing and shoved him straight into the grave. 'Now I've got you!' I shouted. You should have seen how fast he tried to get out. Since that time he won't set foot in the cemetery but calls out from behind the fence."

We looked at the man, who was still hammering away at the fence with his fists and repeating the same sentence over and over again.

My father clenched his fists and shouted: "You'll be six feet under before Easter!"

"Not on your life, I'm as fit as a fiddle."

"You've got a whole cake-tin full of medicines at home. You won't last till Sunday. I'm already working on your grave — it's nearly ready."

"I'll still be frisking about when you're a goner."

"If you hurry up you'll get a spot next to a fetching wench."

Vreugdenhil turned abruptly to his horse and cart, climbed on to the box and with lots of rattling set the cart, which was filled with vegetable peelings and old bread, in motion.

"He even does quite nicely out of that," my father said, more to himself than to anyone else, and after they began to deal again with the stubborn slab he continued to grumble about the strident exchange with the scraps collector.

The stone still refused to budge. Sometimes it would move a fraction of an inch, but by no means always in the right direction, so that the progress made in a quarter of an hour was frequently undone in a few seconds. This occasioned a good deal of cursing in the Lord's name.

"It's no good, Pau," said van Leeuwen. "We'll have to tackle it differently."

"Yes, you're right. If we carry on this way we'll still be here next week. If you ask me, they stuck lead on that grave, and you can bet your boots there'll be an oak or lead coffin. Then the corpse will be as fresh as a daisy and we'll look right silly. Same thing happened to me the other day. This woman comes along and asks, 'Where's my husband buried?' I look it up for her and show her where he is but there's no gravestone on the grave, just two other stones. 'Is this where he is buried?' she asks. 'Yes,' I say. 'But who else is buried here as well?' 'Well, he's nicely buried between two ladies — couldn't wish for better.' Well, she moved heaven and earth to get her husband shifted; on no account could he stay where he was. I even said to her: 'It's not as if it's mixed bathing, is it?' but that didn't help in the slightest; she put up a sackful of shekels to get him shifted, meaning I had to dig him up and stick him somewhere else, and it was a deal coffin in mint condition and as heavy as lead."

"I need a bigger crowbar. I'll just go and get one," said Ai van Leeuwen. "If that doesn't work you'll have to get the council — they've got cranes, haven't they?"

"Yes, but the whole place would be completely flattened by the time you got one of them in here."

"What else would you suggest?"

"We'll break it up."

"Not on your life, not a slab like that: I can get two new stones out of that."

He walked off, pressing his grossly undersized hat down on his skull from time to time. He zigzagged between the plots and sometimes the gravestones would obscure the lower half of his body so that he appeared to waft over the paths like a blue angel with a small hat on. I could not resist looking at him, not only because he was pursuing such an erratic course but because he was walking so slowly, probably out of cautiousness — for to have walked more briskly in the gusty, almost stormy wind would have been fatal for his precariously balanced hat. Walking there he was to me the very essence of adulthood, incomprehensible and forming an ineluctable part of a totally different world, a world differing from my father's, who was so much closer to me. I was quite sure I would never want to belong to Ai van Leeuwen's world, and yet I suspected that, by being present at the exhumation, I was drawing closer to that world. I wanted to leave but not quite yet, for I was alone with my father now, and it did not matter as much. I walked slowly over to the stone and gave it a push — a gesture that was so totally absurd but also so completely natural, that I could not understand why my father should be bellowing.

"Want to move it all by yourself?" he roared cheerfully.

"No, not me," I replied, "but you never can tell."

I kicked against one of the concrete beams supporting the stone, as if to test its hardness and in order to kick away my discomposure. No sooner had I done so than I felt the beam give a little and I kicked it a second time, clenching my fists in my pockets. Then three things happened at once: my father dragged me roughly out of the way with one hand, the concrete beam tilted and the stone began to slip forward hesitantly. My father pushed against the stone with his white clog but to no avail. The stone slab slid forward inexorably, not smoothly but jerkily and uncertainly as if it were stuttering. Sometimes it appeared to have stopped and then it would begin to move again, apparently in another part of the stone. But that could only be an optical illusion; a stone is a stone and if it moves the whole stone moves evenly. But it did not seem like that, possibly because the straggly shadows formed by the shoots on the miserable little tree just behind the gravestone were moving unevenly in the opposite direction to that of the slab. And then, as the stone so erratically moved and stopped moving, a greyish-white patch appeared on the slab just above the verse, and that patch, which was just a bird-dropping, marked the spot where the stone broke in two a moment later. The section with the rhyme fell with a thud on to the path while the other half continued to slide forward as though nothing had happened and landed on the now immobile section, gliding calmly until it too came to rest, as though it had all been pre-arranged, the two stones neatly piled on top of one another; with the point at which they were to break indicated, as if from on high, by a greyish-white mark. We gazed speechlessly at the self-propulsion of the slab. But I was not granted much time for amazement because what had been revealed between the concrete beams where the stone had been was at least as gripping. Hundreds of little animals scuttled off between completely colourless grass — sowbugs, centipedes, beetles and two lethargic toads. I even saw worms. They had apparently ventured up to the surface of the earth in this cool, moist spot and were suddenly exposed to bright sunlight. They tried to wriggle into the ground as quickly as possible, and I thought: *Don't bother, in a moment you'll be dug up by my father anyway.* All the creatures were intent on finding shade. I had never seen so much life together before, so many centipedes and sow-bugs careering about aimlessly. But who would have thought that there would even be toads there?

"That's great, that is," said my father. "Stone broken. When van Leeuwen gets back he'll stamp on his hat in rage; he'll never be able to get two goods stones out of it now. Perhaps he'll be able to get two small stones for children's graves out of it. Well, we'll see. At least the stone's off now."

My father slowly eased out the concrete beams with his crowbar. Each movement of his hands precipitated a new flurry of activity as he altered the position of the shadows. And when he began digging out the sods of white grass I saw fresh swarms of life scurrying off. It was as though the earth beneath his hands was coming to life: as though he were tussling with life itself instead of with death. I carried the sods to a small, unused corner of the cemetery, piling them up carefully so as to cause as little disturbance as possible to those moist, square worlds below my hands.

When my father began to scoop away the sand from where the sods of grass had been, I became aware of a curious tension in my body that seemed suspiciously like fear. I stared at each shovelful of sand, but I did not wish to; I wished instead to look at the scudding clouds, the pipes suspended in the air at Key & Kramer, and the birds building their nests so exuberantly: but no account was taken of what I wished. I could not help looking at the quiet, steady way in which my father scooped out shovelful upon shovelful. And yet it was nothing but sand that was spreading out slowly on top of the heap that now reached to the lower branches of the tree. What would happen next? Would my father strike the coffin? Or would it have rotted away? In that case wouldn't small bits of wood be dug up? But I saw no bits of wood, just grey sand containing little white shells that rolled down more swiftly than the grains of sand as my father scooped out each shovelful. Perhaps nobody had ever been buried here — at least I hoped so. But what about the stone? Perhaps it had simply been shifted to make room elsewhere.

"There's nothing there, is there?" I said manfully to my father. "It's completely empty; just sand."

"Oh, is it?" said my father. "What's this then?"

He scrabbled in the sand and brought out something in his fist which he thrust into my hand. I left it on my hand as it was, except that I opened my hand as wide as possible. In the palm of my hand lay a small, reddish bone. It looked just like a bone from a chop, except that it was moist in a different way and had sand clinging to it. But no matter how much it resembled something I was familiar with I trembled so violently that the bone itself wobbled in my hand. This had belonged to a person, to the man in the verse, and I would be like that one day too, I suddenly knew. There was no room for any other thought.

"There, you see," my father said.

I wanted to reply but was unable to. The words were present somewhere but so thick and full that they failed to move. My tongue felt completely swollen, filling every corner of my mouth until it pressed against my utterly dry palate. I felt a wild, stabbing pain in my stomach and then words came out after all, like very thick treacle — words which it seemed to take hours to get out, into the wind. Nor did I dare open my mouth properly because the wind wanted to go in and blow me up until I burst.

"I'm going away," I stammered.

"Yes, you go away," said my father quietly.

But I was unable to move and simply stood there, shuddering so violently that it was nothing short of a miracle that the bone remained lying on my hand. I knew it would help if I were able to throw it away but I did not dare; nor was I able to, since it had been a person's bone. My father took the bone from my hand and placed it on the heap, throwing sand over it. Then he took me by the hand — the hand that had not touched the bone — and led me carefully across the paving stones. I let myself be led along unprotestingly, although my feet scarcely wished to move.

"You look as white as a sheet," he said quietly. "You'd better go home quickly."

He did not let go of my hand until we reached the gate and I walked very slowly on the pavement past the wire mesh. I realized that I was walking just as slowly as Ai van Leeuwen and I did not wish to, but was unable to walk any faster. I held my hand out in front of me, opened wide; there was still sand stuck to it. If I could just rinse it as quickly as possible there was a chance I might be able to close it again. As I was walking along Ai van Leeuwen came back in his car. He waved to me but I was unable to use my right hand; I had to hold it out in front of me until I had washed it thoroughly. I tried to wave with my left hand but he had already passed and in any case my left hand refused to move.

10

Flight from the 3rd of October

I left my rage behind in the Binntal. Back in Leiden I settled into a
state of mind which, for want of a better term, I described as
resignation and which led me to shrug my shoulders whenever I was in
front of a mirror as though I wanted to say to someone: there's nothing
I can do about it. That sense of resignation, if that was what it was, did
however open my eyes to the music of Richard Strauss in his final
years. I listened over and over again to his four "Letzte Lieder" and to
his "Metamorphosen", and each time I would think: *It's as though he
composed that after he died.*

Perhaps my resignation was nothing more than the absence of rage
— the rage that had been such an effective weapon against death. Now
that I felt resigned death seemed much closer again and I had to come
to terms with it afresh. This led me to do something for reasons I
myself did not fully understand. On the eve of the anniversary of the
Relief of Leiden I rang my father and asked him if I might come and
rake leaves the next day. Why did I want to do that? My father too was
curious and could not understand why I should want to come and do
such humdrum work. I was no clearer than he was why I wanted to,
simply saying: "I thought you might be able to use some help since
you are not quite well again."

"Not quite well again? I'm as healthy as ten others. I beat the lot of
them at billiards at the fire brigade and make short work of my brother
Klaas too."

"I used to enjoy it so much," I said.

"No you didn't," he said. "You did it because you used to get a
quarter for each bag from the florist."

"I want to get out of Leiden tomorrow," I said. "They're
celebrating the 3rd of October tomorrow, which I can't stand —
oompah music, a procession and a fair — and so I thought I'd go and

rake leaves with my father for old times' sake and get away from all those people hovering about the raw herring stalls."

"If you just stayed at home you wouldn't be disturbed, would you?"

"Yes, I would, because you can hear the bands and all sorts of noisy people go past the house all day."

"Well, it wouldn't bother me but if you really want to come naturally I won't stop you. There're nearly six inches of chestnut leaves in the fourth class and you've got my blessing if you want to get rid of them."

And so the next day I walked across to the fourth class with the long rake over my shoulder and I thought: *Why should I want so much to rake up leaves again?* As I looked around at the autumn colours and smelled the scent of rotting and humus, and saw the peaceful, tired, gold-coloured sunlight shining between the trees, I knew that part of the reason for my presence was because it was easiest here to come to terms with death, among the gravestones still standing in mist up to their bottom letters. Just above the ground there was a dividing line between the sun and the mist, a border that seemed a floating surface on which the whole cemetery was drifting. Everywhere I looked I saw leaves falling on to the surface and disappearing beneath it as if they were drowning.

I raked up the leaves on the ground. I thought: now, today, would be the time to begin telling my father of his illness. I need not tell him everything, but something, so that he can start coming to terms with it while he is still able to walk about here in the cemetery. Here it is all of no account: here death cannot be said to be a threat, here death is so natural: gravestones, coffins, funerals, other people's mourning. With each stroke of the rake across the grass death seemed to draw closer and to become more ordinary. I raked up to the Jewish section, where I suddenly saw something that astonished me so much that I threw down the rake in the grass and went to find my father. He was rubbing back a white gravestone among the second-class rental graves but came with me straight away and we both looked at the three young little-owls which were sitting on the bottom-most branch of a chestnut tree.

"They're very late," I said.

"It's the second brood," said my father.

Their plumage was still downy. The two outside owls looked like marble, as though they were old-fashioned bookends holding up the little-owl in the middle, which was the biggest of the three. There they sat, stock-still, staring with large, astonished eyes at the moss-covered, sagging stones in the Jewish plot. As I looked at them, I thought in surprise: *So that is why I came, because I want to tell my father what is wrong. Because I can no longer bear the burden by myself and want to be rid of the secret. Or because I want to prepare him so that he will be more able to cope with it once it reaches that stage?* I tried to convince myself that the latter was the case but knew I was deceiving myself, that I had only come in order to shrug off the secret — to shout it out if necessary, right there in front of those three little-owls. But I did not get the opportunity of saying a single word for as we were standing there a man came up whom we soon recognized as the oldest undertaker in Maassluis. Even at a distance his enormous chin stood out: a chin that had frightened me as a boy because it resembled an axe. When the undertaker spoke it looked as if he were chopping.

"Well, nothing to do today then?" he asked us.

"We were just looking at these little-owls," my father said.

"No mileage in that," he said. "I've got a funeral for you the day after tomorrow — John 19 the last part of verse 41."

"Go on! A first- or second-class private grave?"

"First-class."

"First-class? What a nuisance — you know what Ecclesiastes 4.6 says, don't you?"

"Right — you just read Proverbs 3.30."

"What time's the funeral planned for?"

"Mark 15, the first part of verse 25."

"At three o'clock? You usually come at two."

"That's what the family wants. I can't help it."

"Who is it?"

"Tuitel. He's been ill for six months, as you know."

"I thought he was down for the cookery centre."

"Yes, but they happened to hear a sermon on the radio on Sunday by Reverend Meijnen, who said that cremation was against the Word."

"I'll be blowed! Meijnen — he's been here himself: an aunt of his is buried here. He had been preaching beforehand in Schiedam, so I had gone there on my bike because...."

"Yes, I know, he's the cat's pyjamas."

"Exactly. So off I went, and he preached on Peter's mother-in-law, who was in bed with a fever. Magnificent sermon. The following week he was preaching in Vlaardingen. Off I go again on my bike. What did he preach about? Peter's mother-in-law in bed with a fever. And the next week he preached here. What was the sermon about? You guessed it: Peter's mother-in-law in bed with a fever. Well, the next day he came to the cemetery to visit his aunt's grave and asked me where she was buried. I looked it up and walked with him to the second class and we passed a panel that still had flowers on it from the burial the Saturday before and I say to him: 'Do you know who's buried there, Reverend?' 'No,' he said. 'Peter's mother-in-law,' I say. 'She was in bed with a fever for three weeks and then passed away.' You should have seen his face!''

The undertaker laughed in such a strange way that I feared for the muscles with which his chin was suspended. But he suppressed his laughter and said: "I really wanted to have a word with you, Pau. There's no need for your son to be present."

"You mean you don't want him to hear all the cunning schemes you've got in mind."

"He's welcome to stay, it's no secret; but ignorance is bliss, isn't it?"

"If it's so important I'd rather he stayed. Isaiah 1.15 might well have been written specially for you."

"You can't mean that, Pau. We've always got on so well together."

"You always got on well with Vreugdenhil too, and you know what's become of him."

"I never really worked with Vreugdenhil; my old man did, but at that stage I was just an *aanzegger* in my father's business."

He turned to me with a sly grin and stuck his chin out even more. If he were to give a woman a passionate kiss, it occurred to me, there would be a good chance he'd chop off her head.

"I began as an *aanzegger* when I was ten years old," he told me, "at first only when I had to go around telling people about the death of a child. I was a child *aanzegger*, in two senses. I used to look splendid as a little boy in my top hat and black suit. It's a pity so few children die these days and that the custom of bearing the bad tidings has disappeared, because my grandson is just cut out for the job. Yes, I've been in the trade for over sixty years. Last year I celebrated my jubilee and was given this."

He took a shiny, marble lighter out of his pocket and handed it to me. "It's a pity I don't smoke," he said. "I don't use it, but it's very fine."

I looked at the lighter and thought in amazement: *Sometimes things happen which you have read about in a book and which you thought at the time could not possibly be true.* In *Oliver Twist* there is something to the effect of "he thrust his finger into the snuff-box, which was an ingenious little model of a patent coffin". Meanwhile I looked at the marble lighter which was shaped like a small gravestone, and on which two intertwined branches were depicted above Rest in Peace.

He said: "Got it from the United Stonemasons Federation when I celebrated my sixtieth anniversary." He took the lighter out of my hands and said to my father: "If we just go across to the mortuary for a talk we can leave your son by himself here with the . . . er, what did you say they were?"

"Little-owls," I said.

"What do you want to do," my father asked me, "come to the mortuary or keep on raking?"

"I'll just keep on raking," I said.

"Your son knows Ecclesiastes 1.18," the undertaker said, jutting out his chin.

They walked off and I gathered up old leaves to make way for the falling ones. I thought: *How on earth am I to broach the subject with him if other people keep on turning up? And yet,* I thought, *he ought to know something — he ought to some extent to be prepared, now he is still well and it is still autumn.* I looked towards my father, who was disappearing into the mortuary with his companion. The sun was shining on his head and, compared with the undertaker, he still looked so young. I tried to imagine what it would be like to be told you didn't have long to live. But I was unable to conceive of it, and could only think of the poem "Since I have known" by Jacqueline van der Waals. Would it be as she says in the poem? Would the same apply to my father, being so religious as he was: "Since I have known my God is close to me?" If that were so, was I allowed to remain silent; was it not my duty to say something to him? For did she not go on to write:

> Since I have known my God is close to me.
> Often, lost in our earthly games and trials,
> I unexpectedly will feel His smile
> Steal over me with rare intensity.

But how could I be sure that my father would respond in exactly the same way as Jacqueline van der Waals? The fact that I identified so closely with her when I read her work — although I would never be able to write such poetry — did not guarantee that my father would feel any such identification with or even affinity for her poetry. But perhaps he already knew, as she had already known:

> For we are only too inclined
> To shun such words as seem unkind
> Or rough and slightly harsh in sound.

Yes, that was it. I had been only too inclined to avoid even alluding to it, and perhaps I was only raking leaves in order to put a stop to it. But what would I gain from telling him? For me, nothing would change, but for him, everything. And yet I wanted to be rid of the secret and to talk about it — not just with anyone, but with my father.

There was not the slightest opportunity of saying anything to my father that day. I raked up leaves and my father showed visitors around, being forced on one occasion to enlist the aid of his dentures in getting rid of a lady who was complaining vociferously that he was disturbing the peace of the graveyard with his motor-mower.

At the end of the day I walked home with him, tired out by the unfamiliar work. The walk was far too brief for any sort of conversation. Moreoever I felt quite unable to raise the subject with him once we were beyond the cemetery gate. In the cemetery itself there would have been a real possibility. I could have asked him about his father's grave or I could have used Peter's mother-in-law as a pretext for discussing his father-in-law's death. But that would have had to have happened in the cemetery.

When we reached my parents' house my father said to my mother: "All these blasted people kept on coming up to me today," and when he was sitting next to the stove with a cup of coffee he told her: "Who should turn up this morning but Jojé Langeveld, wanting to hatch some plot or other. Wanted to discuss it privately with me, didn't even want Mart around, did he, Mart?"

"No," I said.

"Well, off I go with him to the mortuary. Do you know what he wanted? You'll never guess. 'Paulus,' the old rogue says to me, 'you and I often hear of people who've lost a relative and who are looking for a gravestone. Well, now, there's this new stonemason's yard in Schiedam — a big business with ten employees — and they're prepared to give us a good cut if we recommend them all the time. And listen, Pau, if we work as a team, if all those mourners get to hear from both you and me that there's this decent stonemason in Schiedam, orders for nice headstones will come tumbling in.' 'And what about van Leeuwen?' I asked. 'We'll squeeze van Leeuwen right out of business. The two of us — or three or four of us if possible, because I'm going to talk with my colleagues as well — can sneeze him right out,' he says. 'And for what reason?' I ask. 'Did van Leeuwen ever give you a cut if you advised someone to order a gravestone from him?' he says. 'I've never advised anybody to go to van Leeuwen. I always tell everyone they're round the twist to stick a stone on a grave, it's a gravedigger's biggest bugbear,' I say. 'Well,' he says, 'we'll be getting ten per cent from that Schiedammer. Perhaps you won't sneeze at that but will be prepared to overlook your dislike of gravestones.' 'What a grasping old bugger you are,' I say to him, 'haven't you made enough yet? You're well over seventy.' 'I can do with it, just like you and everyone else. I'm not one to pass up an opportunity. Nor did Our Lord and Saviour object when Mary bathed his feet with precious oil, and it's nice to think you might be able to leave something of an inheritance. But van Leeuwen has never given me a thing. He just says that he recommends me and that it goes without saying that I'll recommend him. But if you ask me he doesn't recommend me at all — it's a pack of lies. Oh, Pau, how I'd love to squeeze him out,' he says. 'Oh, so that's what it's all about, is it?' I say. 'Well, and what of it? Look here, you can't do a deal with the bloke...' he says. 'Yes, that's just what I like about him,' I say. 'So you won't join in?' he asks. 'Not on your life,' I say. Well, he jumped up like a bunch of fleas and says: 'You'll never do a deal either, you and van Leeuwen are a pair of pious hypocrites.' 'If the cap fits, you'll get a sore head,' I say to him, and he kept on abusing me for a while, even telling me that I didn't know Malachi 3 verses 8 to 10 properly. 'Do you really think,' I say to him, 'that I didn't know what it says? "Bring ye all the tithes into the storehouse." But it's not the money you're after,' I say to him. 'You want to stick your knife into van Leeuwen — a man who has always worked here as honest as the day is long and who's always prepared to give me a hand to lift or move a stone even though he knows I tell everyone on no account and whatever they do not to stick a stone on a grave. I suppose you thought,' I told him, 'you might as well try — nothing ventured, nothing gained. Well, just as long as you know that I'll never recommend you again to anyone. I suppose you thought Pau is poor and I'm a deceiver and if those two meet the Lord will lighten both their eyes, as it says in Proverbs 29.13, but in that case you got the wrong end of the stick. No, my friend, that one won't wash; you better try peddling your wares somewhere else.'"

My mother sliced the bread and my father got up and went to sit down at the dining-table. I followed him and my father and mother folded their hands while he prayed:

"O Father, source of all life's needs,
Thy blessing on this meal bestow.
Help us to shun excess and greed
And Thy commands and will to know.
We thank Thee for these mercies, Lord,
Extended by Thy bounteous Hand.
Sustain our souls through Thy true Word,
That we Thy ways might understand."

I wondered: *How does God like being addressed in verse?* Does he appreciate the art of poetry at all or know how much it can mean to someone if death is in prospect? *No*, I thought, *He can't understand anything of it because He knows nothing about death. He never died and will never die, but He let His Son fix things up vicariously, staying nicely out of range Himself.* Vicarious suffering, I thought; yes, the vicarious suffering of Christ: but he was not replacing us but his Father. *No, God*, I thought, *you don't understand a thing about poetry.* I thought of the months that had passed, of the poems that had continually flitted through my mind, of the poem by Jacqueline van der Waals and of the other poem, The Poem, and it was all as Postma had written: a father, a mother, a child, and the night was indeed stealing around the silent house and we kept still as though we were listening and perhaps we were each caught in our separate dreams. But it was not the time to roam until after we had eaten and I would certainly have gone to the harbour if my father had not suggested a game of chess. We set up the pieces and as usual my father said:

"All I need is to get both your knights. Once I've got them I'll win."

We played and he kept on pursuing my knights until at last he took them. I felt astonished that I could only counter with a feeble defence and, after he had won the first game, he said: "It's too much that I can even beat you at chess when I'm buggered if I know how to play it. Just think what would happen if we played draughts, which I can play — it's just that I can't stand joining a draughts club or I'd wipe that Koepermann off the board just like that; and you, with your brains, should be able to beat me at chess!"

During the second game he began talking about his father as though he knew I had been thinking of his father's grave that day. I was regaled with a long story over the chessboard, with his hand hovering over the board with a pawn from time to time.

"After a fire my father bought up the entire contents of a sawmill, thousands of clogs with black scorch marks, and had them delivered to Maassluis by barge. My brothers had to unload them at Veer Street: there were three barrow-loads of clogs and my father bellowed to my brothers, 'Make sure you sell them all over the place!' and after a week or two nearly all of them had been sold. We just had a dog-cart full left. Then my father said to me one Saturday afternoon, 'We're off to Maas Dyke.' I was about six years old at the time. Well, we set off along the dyke with those blasted clogs and with that old, black dog, which my father wouldn't get rid of or replace, the stingy, greedy old bastard, pulling the cart, and then we sold all those clogs on the Maas Dyke. A pair of the clogs with blackened noses — they looked just like a burnt match — for forty-five cents, five pairs for two-fifty, as the sly old skinflint called out everywhere — and all sorts of people even bought five pairs of those burnt match-heads — and when we'd finished the old villain said to me, 'Right, I'm getting on the cart and you can give me a push,' and then I pushed him all the way home, together with that dog, which should have been pensioned off long ago. Five kilometres it was and he, a man of forty, sat on the cart while I, a boy of just six, pushed it."

After a move or two came the moral of the story: "As I was walking there I said to myself: 'When I've got children I'll treat them quite differently."

As he was saying that a bishop remained poised above the board and his hand froze.

"And yet," he said, "I used to beat you. For years on end I used to thump the daylights out of you every night."

"I think you're starting to lose," I said.

"No," he said, and he got up and walked over to the stove to put on some more coal.

"In just a few more years," he said, "you won't have to do that any more. Then all you'll need to do is open a small door in the front and pop one of those little atoms —" he screwed up one of his eyes as though he were peering at something that was really too small to be seen — "in the stove and you can leave it to burn from October to Christmas without having to touch it."

"Nonsense," I said. "You'd be much better off with a gas-fire. Who burns coal these days?"

"I'm waiting for the atom," my father said.

"Not in your lifetime," I said.

"Don't you think so?" he said, suddenly alert. "Do you think I'll kick the bucket as soon as that?"

"Not that quickly," I said as innocently as possible. "But it will take decades before we can do anything with nuclear energy and you needn't imagine that you would ever be able to stick a little atom in the stove."

"By that time they will. But listen, do you really think I'm not going to last all that long?"

"Whatever makes you think that?"

"I don't know. I just feel uneasy."

"What about?"

"The operation."

"If you were really in a bad way you wouldn't be playing chess like you are now."

"You might be letting me win on purpose. I used to let my father beat me at draughts on purpose too."

"Yes, when he was over eighty."

"All right, I'm not as old as that, but perhaps you know more than I do and are letting me win for that reason."

"What would I know more about?"

"About that operation."

He looked at me and suddenly burst out laughing. "Don't look so serious," he said. "Can't you see I'm having you on? I'm just pulling your leg because I can see you're doing your level best to beat me, and even so you can't."

"You really must drop that nonsense about the atom," I said. "Nobody will ever be able to put a little atom in a stove — that's arrant nonsense. Whatever gave you that idea?"

"Well, well, well," he said with perverse delight to my mother, "making heavy weather of things today. About to lose again to his old father, even though he studied for six years."

"Who says you're my old father?" I said. "Do I need to remind you again of Reverend Duursema's sermon? You know quite well what he said: 'You can always be sure your Heavenly Father is your father but you can never be sure about your own father; that's a matter of faith.'"

"I know, you'd be pretty pleased, wouldn't you, if I wasn't your father? Wouldn't have to be ashamed of such a bumpkin. But whose eyes have you got then? If I look in the mirror or your mug I see just the same eyes. And where do you think you got your brains?"

"From my mother," I said. "If I were really a son of yours I would only be able to play draughts and chess and billiards and to sand stones down so smooth that the letters were completely gone."

"Yes, I'll be dealing with another one tomorrow morning: start again tomorrow with fresh reluctance."

"Why with fresh reluctance? I though you were allowed to heave out all the stones from the third class?"

"Yes, that's nice but I don't enjoy it any more. Ever since the operation I feel as though I'm working for myself; I'd like to do something else. Best of all I'd like to do some farming till I retire."

He moved a rook and shouted, "Mate!" but that proved not to be so. But I resigned since there was no point in playing on. He leapt exultantly to his feet and walked through the house, seemingly years younger than I was.

"I should never have left the market-garden," he said.

"But for all that your work has given you great pleasure for years," I said.

"It doesn't give me any pleasure now. I wish I were working in the garden and that you were walking all the way to meet me again."

"Do you still remember that?" I asked in amazement.

"Do I remember that? Of course I remember that — you were still such a little chap, could hardly pee over the end of your little clogs, and yet you walked to meet me, all the way from Maassluis. You came to meet me, even though I beat and kicked you every night."

11

Enoch

My first memories of death are of the stream of urine that appeared from under the black pall, eddying and bubbling its way down the gutter into the drain. The pall hung down on either side of the horse's back to just above the ground; here and there the fringe grazed the cobblestones. The urine hissed out from between the tassels of the fringe. Near the pall it was still light yellow but it became steadily darker as it flowed towards the drain. Bubbles were floating on the surface, some of which popped before they emerged from under the pall, while others easily reached the drain. I could not see which of the two horses in front of the black coach was responsible for the urine. One of the horses snorted and threw back its head, to which two black plumes had been affixed which shook to and fro. I expected them to fall off at any moment. Perhaps I even hoped they would. The horse scraped a hoof over the cobblestones and the sparks flew up much more visibly than usual because it was so dark beneath the covered backs of those horses, and I thought: *That horse is doing it.* I bent down and tried to see something of their bellies between the wheels of the coach, and in the gloom I did in fact vaguely make out the outline of the unusually large organ that was spraying urine on to the street. But it was not the snorting horse pawing the ground that was producing the stream; no, it was the other, motionless horse that was urinating, and which kept on passing water as if it wished to douse the fire that its neighbour's hoof was extracting from the street, and it was something to remember for ever: the red sparks flickering in the gloom next to the urine, which boiled as though it had a life of its own, and the neighing of the horse that was not urinating; and added to all that the unreal quietness of all the people standing around, who neither spoke nor moved but just waited for the moment when the coffin would emerge from the house of our neighbour, Mr Kraan. What that signified, I did not know — he was gone, that was all. As long as I could remember he used to sit at his work-bench, framed in green begonias in the window of the front room and, with his bald skull gleaming red in the late afternoon sun, he would form a large and impressive figure. He never used to look up when you peered inside but just kept hammering away at all the shoes from the entire neighbourhood which he re-soled or re-heeled. The shoes were no longer to be seen because a white sheet had been hung in the window, just as in every other window in our street. In our house too there was a freshly-laundered sheet that cast a strange, quiet half-light over the room, exhorting one to whisper rather than to speak, and that made laughing or smiling impossible.

The urinating had stopped but I remained bent forward because that enormous, scarcely visible organ was slowly shrivelling up; it looked as though it was being hoisted up. As I peered intently I suddenly heard a voice: "You should be ashamed of yourself."

I looked round in fright. Uncle Job towered high about me, looking at me with flickering eyes through his spectacles.

"Off you go, beat it. Where are your manners?"

I got up but did not go away. Give way to Uncle Job? If I were to tell my father he would be furious. I stood there, just as quiet as all the others: as our neighbour Van Baalen, who was wearing a black silk cap, as Jannetje Smoor, clad despite the death in a red-hemmed petticoat beneath her black dress, as Kareltje van Wolferen, who even now was dressed from top to toe in a brown leather coat and a brown leather cap that only revealed two beady eyes; as our neighbour Mr Admiraal, and Japie Voogd, the latter already drunk despite the fact that it had only just struck one, although on this occasion he was not singing one of his own songs about the sea and drink and money; and like Uncle Job, who was still wearing his white butcher's coat and thus stood out against the others. Yes, they were all standing there and I saw Mr Van Baalen respectfully doffed his cap when the coffin was carried out and placed in the leading coach. Mrs Kraan followed the coffin in the same staid black she always wore, and yet there was a difference. On Sundays when she went to church she would wear a coloured feather in her hat but this time even the feather was black and each time Mrs Kraan moved the feather moved in the sunlight like a busy bird. I could not take my eyes off it until she disappeared into the coach and the cortege moved off. But how slowly it all went, seeming to take hours before the procession had left the street and began to go up the ramp leading to the dyke. When it eventually disappeared from view people all at once began talking loudly and Uncle Job, who was still next to me, began swearing at me and twisted my ear round with his right hand because I had stooped down to see the horse urinating.

I ran home, defied the grey light cast by the sheet in the window, and called out to my mother: "They've gone and Uncle Job swore at me and wrenched my ear because I wanted to look at the horse...."

"Don't take any notice of Uncle Job."

"Where is Mr Kraan now?"

"In heaven."

"But what about the coffin?"

"Yes, his body is in the coffin but his soul is in heaven with the Lord God. When you die your soul leaves the body."

"Oh," I paused for a moment and then asked: "Does that sheet have to stay up?"

"Yes, until this evening."

I suddenly felt so distressed at the idea of the oppressive half-light remaining in the house so much longer and so depressed that Uncle Job had sworn at me that I longed to see my father. If only he were there everything would be all right. But now — those horses, the coffin, the black feather. Strange: the coffin had been less sad than the black feather and the two pairs of black plumes on the horses' heads.

"I'm going to the allotment," I blurted out.

"To the allotment? All by yourself? Impossible. You're much too little."

"I'm not little at all and I know exactly where it is."

"It's an hour and a half's walk and you don't know the way."

"I do know the way — you just go to the dyke and then go along it to Marie's house where it turns the corner and then you go to the Tin Shed and then it's a little further to the Toll Gate where you leave the dyke and go up Westgaag. And then you just keep on walking until you're there."

"Are you sure you won't get lost?"

"I've been there lots of times, haven't I?"

"Yes, but never by yourself."

"Well, what does that matter? I can find it, don't worry."

"Suit yourself. But don't you talk to strangers and, whatever you do, don't take a lift from any men. Promise you won't? If they say, 'I'll give you a ride some of the way on my bicycle,' you just shake your head as hard as you can, even if you know the man quite well."

"Even if it's Uncle Job?"

"Yes, even then. Be careful, keep walking, pay attention. The Toll Gate, that's the hardest — how will you find that?"

"I can find it," I said earnestly, "because it's the only spot along the dyke where there are two ramps in the same place."

She looked at me and I saw the pride in her eyes.

"You really are quick-witted," she said. "Well, off you go, but don't accept any sweets, not from anybody, and don't let anyone give you a lift."

And so I ascended the steps past the sewage station in the windy spring air and walked along the dyke towards my father's allotment. *It's quiet easy,* I thought: *you just keep walking along the dyke until you reach the Toll Gate. The Toll's the only difficult thing where I'll need to keep an eye out.* From time to time I looked round because I kept on thinking: *In a minute she'll follow me to stop me going after all.* But she did not come and nor was Uncle Job to be seen anywhere in the fields or on the road. But I did see the funeral coaches, which were apparently already returning from the funeral. Or were they different coaches? They were proceeding ahead of me along the dyke, which almost made my trip superfluous, since it was from those very coaches and horses that I had been fleeing. But also from that quiet half-light. The coaches left the dyke at the descent near Weverskade, where they stopped near a large coach-house, and when I saw them down in the depths from on top of the dyke, I knew I had been right to flee from them. I left them behind me, even though the bend in the dyke meant that they remained visible for a long time if I looked back. The further I got, the more innocent they appeared, for the palls were taken off the horses' backs, the plumes removed and the horses unhitched. It had less and less to do with death, and increasingly became a perfectly ordinary scene of two horses and two coaches. The horses were driven into a meadow and the coaches pushed inside the coach-house one by one and there seemed nothing left to prevent my returning home. But I had already come such a long way — Marie's house was looming up, besides which there was such a fragrance in the air and the sky was such a beautiful blue, and the clouds were scudding past in the sky at such wonderful speed.

All at once I saw that black feather before me again. What would it be like to die? Or would I never die? No, I would not die; I would continue to live until the Lord Jesus returned in the clouds of heaven, and would be taken up to heaven just like that, one, two, three, alive and well, just like my father and my mother. Or perhaps, if I did not live long enough to experience Christ's second coming, I would become a man of God like the prophet Elijah and ascend to heaven with fiery horses and fiery chariots in a whirlwind. But before that point was reached I would have to live a very long time to become a man of God. I would have to become very old, like our neighbour Mr Kraan.

"Well, young fellow, going for a walk all by yourself?"

I looked up. A friendly, not-so-young man was cycling next to me, looking at me with a smile.

"Where are you going?"

"To my father."

"Where is your father?"

"At Mrs Poot's garden in Westgaag."

"What's your father called?"

"Pau."

"What, are you one of Pau and Lena's sons!"

He had to wriggle his front wheel to stop falling over, and I walked even more slowly.

"So you're Arie van der Griessen's grandson. The best market-gardener in the Westland; vegetables always of export quality. Would you like a bit of a ride?"

"No."

"Why not?"

"I'd rather walk."

"Yes, but if I give you a lift you'll reach your father sooner. I know your father, you see — he's the wittiest fellow at the market and always has fine vegetables; only your grandfather's are better. I'm a gardener myself, you see. I've got a plot just by the Toll, so I could take you that far."

I shook my head. That was what I had to do, my mother had said: "Don't speak but shake your head."

"It's up to you. If you don't want to, don't. Regards to your parents."

He rode on, glancing round now and then, smiling and motioning with one hand to his carrier and I kept on shaking my head as he slowly disappeared from sight under those fast-moving clouds. Oh, how splendid they were, those small clouds chasing each other so swiftly ahead of me, as though they were showing me the way. If I keep on walking like this, I thought, I'll reach the Hoek of Holland and then I'll see the sea. How quickly would those clouds reach the sea? I did

128

not know, and looked at the cow parsley on the bank of the dyke swaying in the breeze and at the young willows whisperingly caressed by the wind. I was now level with the house that belonged to Marie, a woman I had never seen who was said to have lived in the house from time immemorial. I had always hoped that she would come outside when I passed the house sitting in front on my father's bicycle.

"What does she look like?" I would ask my father.

"She's old."

"Why do we never see her?"

"She always stays inside."

Now, for the first time, I hoped that she would not come out and I myself did not know why I was suddenly scared of her. I heard the irascible grunting of her invisible pigs as I passed the tumble-down building that was pressed so forlornly up against the dyke. As usual she did not come outside; perhaps she did not exist at all but was dead like Mr Kraan, who was now in heaven with God. That was why those pigs were grunting so crossly. Mr Kraan was high above those scurrying clouds, far beyond the clear blue — with God. But God is everywhere, God could easily be on the dyke — perhaps he even was on the dyke. I loved God with all my heart and all my mind, that I knew for certain, for I heard that every Sunday in the Zuider Church; perhaps I even loved God more than my father and my mother. Perhaps? No, without any doubt. "He that loveth father or mother more than me is not worthy of me", the Lord Jesus had said. God cared for everything, God loved all mankind, loved mankind so much that he had let his own Son be nailed to the cross. You could only love such a God infinitely. Someone who had sacrificed his own Child for your sins. "God," I muttered, "I love you very much," and as I said it, it seemed as though He were walking by my side. No, there was not a soul to be seen on the dyke, as far as the eye could see, but He could appear at any moment and start walking by my side, just as He must have walked next to Enoch. "And Enoch walked with God: and he was not; for God took him." Had my mother perhaps been warning me about God? Was that why she hadn't explained why I shouldn't go with any strange men? God could be one of those strange men and if you loved God a lot He would take you away, just like He had taken Enoch away and then you were no longer there and of course my mother wouldn't want that. Or was she jealous because I loved God more, and indeed had to love God more than her, in order to be worthy of Him? Was that why she didn't want me to go with a stranger, who might be God? If He took me away she would never see me again and then she would be sad and so would my father, I was sure; they would be sad because they definitely loved me more than they loved the Lord God, and that was all right because it didn't say that you were not worthy of God if you loved your children more than Him, no, it just said that you were not worthy of God if you loved father and mother more. Well, then, if God appeared I would explain it all to Him. Lord Jesus, I would say, I don't mind being taken away but that would make my father and mother very sad, so please wait a bit, there's no hurry, and your Father knows how bad it is when things are going wrong with a child. Didn't your Father cry when you were on the cross, and didn't it pierce your Mother's heart?

But God was not yet to be seen on the dyke. The wind was, however, swishing past the clouds and I thought I heard His blessed name, while on the left-hand side of the road the greenery was so high that God could easily linger there without being seen. Yes, the grass was even moving and a man with fiery cheeks rose up out of the cow parsley and a moment later a woman who pulled down her skirt, and I stared in amazement at the woman and her astonishingly blotched complexion. The man suddenly ran towards me. I wanted to run away but I was too late.

He seized me by the arm and snarled: "You shut your trap and keep quiet."

"Yes, yes," I said.

"Promise you won't say anything?"

"No, sir."

"You sure?"

"Yes, sir, I'm sure."

"Remember, if you breathe a word I'll kill you."

He let go of me and then the woman came up. I looked in astonishment at her red cheeks; there was something dull and sad and yet also happy about her face.

She stooped down and smiled at me. "Hello. You won't tell anybody, will you?"

"No, madam," I said.

"That's a big boy. Would you like a sweet?"

"No."

"Why not?"

"I don't like sweets."

"Don't you like sweets? What about an apple?"

"No."

"Why not?"

"My father says they give you the trots."

She laughed merrily and there was something about her face and her eyes above her flushed cheeks that made me very happy. She was more beautiful than any woman I had ever seen, not because her face was so beautiful but because her cheeks were so red that they seemed on fire.

"So you really don't want anything?"

"No, madam, I'm on my way to my father's allotment."

"All by yourself?"

"Yes."

"Who on earth would let a child wander over the dyke all by himself? Really, some people are quite mad. Where is your father's allotment?"

"In the Westgaag."

"That's still a long way."

"No, it's not," I said and walked on, leaving them behind in amazement. I looked round and she waved at me and I waved back, and all at once I knew that I loved her. And yet she could not be God because God was a man. Why did that make me feel sad for a moment? I didn't know, but only knew it had been the glow in her cheeks that had made me love her so suddenly.

In the distance the Tin Shed was gleaming in the sun and when I looked back Maassluis was already a long way off and I could no longer make out the hands on the clock on the tower.

What would God look like? Would He, like those men who had been carrying the coffin, be wearing a black suit? Or would He be all in white like a bride? And a source of light: He could look like a burning bush. But He could of course also appear in disguise and, as I was thinking that, it occurred to me: perhaps that the man on the bicycle was God. He knew what my father and mother were called and knew my grandfather's name and what he did; yes, he knew everything, just like God. But God on a bicycle? That seemed most strange to me; there was nothing about it in the Bible and yet it was by no means impossible because God could do everything. So He would be able to ride a bicycle too. But then that man hadn't looked like God at all; a small, unprepossessing man with a brown deerstalker with a jaunty feather stuck in the band. A black feather — I suddenly pictured it, although at the time I had hardly paid any attention to it: a black feather, just like on Mrs Kraan's hat. Why would that man have worn a black feather in a brown hat if he were not God and knew nothing of the death of our neighbour, Mr Kraan?

A car passed me, disappearing a second later beyond the Tin Shed, which, its roof shimmering painfully, lay glinting in the sun. A cyclist was struggling against the wind on the other side of the road and I thought: if my father were cycling there he could overtake that man in a flash, headwind or no headwind. After the cyclist came a lady on a bicycle who was even more troubled by the wind and near the Tin Shed some small, dark figures were walking in the spring sunshine, while overhead a flight of geese cut across the dyke. Everything seemed imbued with the spirit of God. Yes, he had taken Elijah up into heaven in a fiery chariot but earlier He had appeared to the same Elijah when there had been no wind. Well, it was certainly not windless and that all at once set me at ease — at least He would not appear now, for it was much too windy. What had the weather been like when he took Enoch? The Bible didn't say. He had appeared to Adam, walking in the cool of the evening. It was cool, but it was not evening. Why was I afraid of God? I only had to say to Him, if He should walk beside me: "Lord Jesus, I really do love you more than my father and my mother, but it would upset them so much if you took me away now that perhaps you could wait a little. Enoch was quite old when you took him away, wasn't he?" How old? What a nuisance that I didn't know exactly. Methuselah had lived to 969, the oldest ever — but Enoch? Enoch was Methuselah's father, so at least he couldn't have been taken away as a little child. Enoch walked with God, "And Enoch walked with God: and he was not; for God took him." How? Why didn't the Bible say how it happened? Took him — just like Mr Kraan in a coffin and a coach pulled by two horses, one of which made fire and the other water. Did that mean Mr Kraan had not walked with God?

"You won't find a devouter man than Mr Kraan," I had often heard my mother say. But then he had always just sat there encircled in greenery; he had never walked. God might well have said to him: "Kraan, why don't you go outside for a change and come for a stiff walk," but Kraan had of course replied: "First of all I've got to re-sole that shoe and to stitch up those other shoes, and that one needs a new heel and that one's got to have new laces — no time today." That was why Kraan had been taken away in a coffin and had not been taken up like Enoch. No, I did not want to be put in a coffin but nor did I want to be taken up. Later, perhaps, but not now, not yet. "Just wait a little, God," I prayed. "Please wait a little."

I passed the Tin Shed. The roof was shimmering so brightly in the sunlight that I went past with my head to one side. I looked down across the dyke, over the green buds of the corn poppies that had not as yet come out, towards Janus Hoekveen's little white house in the Weverskade. The crowns of the tall poplars surrounding the house swayed majestically as though they had tamed the wind. On the Weverskade the same man in the brown deerstalker was cycling into the wind. Every now and then he pressed his hat down on his head with one hand, so he obviously was not God, since He naturally didn't need to worry that His hat would blow off. And you could see that it was costing him a lot of effort to pedal into the wind. No, he was definitely not God. God would make the wind change direction or would be able to cycle against it like an angel. Nor would God ride such a rusty old bike. But the man was still wearing the black feather in his hat and he had known everything. God could of course deliberately pretent He was not God to trick me. I stared intently at the cyclist on the Weverskade until it occurred to me that he might look up, however difficult it might be for him to lift his head with the strong wind in his face. And so I disappeared into the tall grass among the flowering lady's smocks and crept a short distance through the stalks of grass up to a willow, where I hid. I could see the man quite clearly but he would not be able to see me if he looked up. And yet — if it were God, there was no point in hiding. He would always see you, even if He were to cycle into the wind a thousand times.

The man had now reached one of the three bridges over the waterway that led to a descent. He stopped at the bridge, lifted his hat, wiped the sweat from his brown and then scanned the dyke, first of all in the direction of the Tin Shed, and then turning round in my direction. I knelt down lower in the grass and peered at him through the green stalks. He kept on staring at the dyke embankment, moving his head from side to side and each time lifting his hat to wipe away the perspiration. I suddenly knew it could not be God: God would know exactly where I was and would not need to gaze up and down the dyke. I was also sure that the man was looking for me, which frightened me, but at the same time there was the comforting thought: *At least it is not God, thank God.*

The man walked up the ramp wheeling his bicycle and came on to the dyke, stared for a long time down the road towards the Tin Shed and then mounted his bicycle and cycled in my direction. I huddled up even smaller behind the willow and he passed by swiftly because he now had the wind behind him and I saw how he was scanning the slope for any sign of life. For a moment it seemed as though he was going to find me, because he hesitated just after he had passed, perhaps because the grass had been flattened on the bank, but he went on, silhouetted on top of the dyke which, from where I was sitting, was just an outline. He skimmed above the strip of grass and the cow parsley; the lower part of his wheels was out of sight and he was whistling an agitated sort of tune that bore no resemblance whatever to a psalm. But in any case I knew now it could not be God. The black feather waved in the wind and I thought: *What should I do now?* I did not dare to leave the protection of the clump of willows, but nor could I keep on lying there. I could not go back: he would always be able to overtake me on his bicycle, despite the headwind. Keep going in the same direction as he was? Certainly not. I slowly crept up the slope through the grass and looked along the dyke, where I saw him disappearing over the white concrete with which the dyke was paved. I did not dare stand up, and in the hazy light, he appeared as a black shadow which, in the distance, was no longer moving but was just growing smaller. He left the dyke by the descent before the one at the Toll Gate. What would he do now? Cycle along the Westerkade again into the wind? I did not wait to see but hastily crossed the dyke and ran along the thick hawthorn hedge until an opening appeared, which I wriggled through. On the other side of the hedge there was a narrow strip of grass between the meadowland and the hawthorn, and I ran down it along the hedge, which screened me from anybody riding or walking on the dyke. The wind was not in my back and I was able to run briskly, but every now and then I would peer out over the dyke through the infrequent gaps in the hedge. I could not see him and kept on running, despite the fact that some people were burning weeds int the distance, which made me think again of the burning bush. I realized that it might well occur to the man that I was walking behind the hawthorn hedge. But I had no choice but to go on; I was now much closer to my father's allotment than to home.

When I drew level with the Toll Gate I stared for a long time through an opening in the hedge. I could not see the man and so crossed the road cautiously, flopped down in the grass on the other side of the dyke and scanned the Weverskade. There was not a cyclist in sight. Nothing but swaying reed along a narrow path. Even so I did not dare get up. I looked up the Westgaag — the winding road lay gleaming quietly in the sun. High reeds were growing in the water on the right-hand side of the road but I would not be able to hide in them. On the left-hand side there was a breathtakingly high, steep slope that had been freshly mown. There, too, I would be unable to get out of sight if the man should happen to follow me. What next? I lay in the grass, the sun shone on me as though nothing was up and everywhere the tree-tops were swaying. Then I saw a small cart in the farmyard to the left of the Toll Gate. For a moment it reminded me of the coaches I had seen earlier that day but the small, fawn pony hitched to the cart in no way resembled those two stately horses. It stood there, its head hanging down, like a statue of a pony, and I recognized the animal before I recognized the cart. Chickens were walking about quietly in the farmyard, a white goose waddled by and for a brief moment a little girl appeared wearing a white pinafore and a ribbon in her hair. I slithered down the slope in the grass, hastily crossed the bridge where the Toll Gate must once have been and sauntered into the yard. Apart from the little girl and the chickens and the goose there were two men. And in the middle of the yard, standing as peacefully as if they had been there for hours, were two pigs. The bigger of the two was leaning on the other one's back and waving its little tail. It almost seemed as if it were embracing the other pig's back with its two forepaws.

One of the men, the older of the two, said to the girl: "You just watch how many times Berend winks and then you'll know exactly how many piglets are coming."

I looked intently at the pig leaning so jauntily on the other's back. His eyes were wide open and he didn't blink his eyelids a single time. Then he suddenly got down and growled indignantly before marching off towards the cart and the old man. The boar-keeper (for I had recognized him now) walked behind him and said: "Well done, old fellow."

The animal grunted by way of reply and jumped straight into the cart from the ground. The boar-keeper shut the little black door and I heard some good-humoured grunting, which the boar-keeper answered with a cheerful laugh. Then he caught sight of me.

"Well, well, what are you doing here? Where's your father?"

"At the allotment."

"How did you get here then?"

"I walked."

"All the way from the allotment?"

"No, from home."

"Do you need to go to the allotment then? Is there something wrong with your mother?"

"No, I just wanted to go and meet my father. Could I ride along with you a little way?"

"Of course, come and sit next to me in the box. Now up you get, first your right foot, then the left; no, put your hand here, yes, that's right, now pull up your other foot; whoa, wait, I'll give you a lift. Now just let me go round the other side; yes, that's the way, well done. There we are, perched up on top like a lord. Now me, and then off we go. Come on you old crock, gee up."

He flapped the reins in the air and the pony lifted its head but did not budge. He flapped the reins again and now the horse hesitantly moved its legs and we plodded into the Westgaag.

"The old fellow's really over the hill. But Berend — you should see Berend — he's still in tremendous form. Well, better that the animal behind me is in form than the one in front — and in any case it lets Berend get his breath back ambling along the Westgaag like this, because I hope he can serve another sow today. Two would probably be too much, but you could manage another one, eh, Berend?" He tapped the van behind him with his left hand.

Once again I heard the contented grunting, which the boar-keeper answered with: "Still getting on pretty well, eh, in your cart? As far as I know there are still two sows on heat, so see what you can do, eh, Berend."

He paused for a moment and then turned to me: "Now what do you think, son of Pau; my wife said to me: 'You should get rid of that dilapidated old cart and buy a car and hook up one of those cattle trailers, and then you could take along two boars instead of one and get lots more done in a day. While one of them was getting its wind back the other could be serving, taking it in turns as it were, and you'd get more done and earn more.' 'Yes,' I said, 'but you needn't think you can stick two boars in the same cart, unless they're brothers who've grown up together from the start.' 'Well, can't you put a partition in the cart?' 'Yes, I suppose I could,' I replied, and it's not a bad idea and yet I can't bear to give up the old van. It's such peaceful and pleasant work, you see, with just one boar, and I make quite a nice living, so what more do I want?"

"I would never get a car," I said.

"There, listen to what a child has to say. I'll have to tell my wife.

Never get a car, there you are. But why not?"

"Well, I think a horse like that's so lovely."

"Would you like to hold the reins for a while?"

He thrust them into my hand and the horse trotted on quietly, unaware that the reins had been transferred.

"That's right, young 'un, all these new-fangled things aren't worth it. Take a car — first of all you've got to pass a driving test, well, and that at my age. I've had my three score years and ten and have got children bigger than I am — Piet, the eldest, is a foot and a half taller than I am. No, this carriage will last me to the grave — hang on, pass me the reins, there's a bicycle coming."

And there he went, the man with the brown deerstalker. Brushing past us. He could easily have tapped me as he went by but he didn't glance at us, just holding on to his hat and wobbling past the little horse, which the man had brought to a halt so that it could be passed. I looked up at the clouds and it seemed as though I could see God sitting on his throne and He too looked at me, astonished because I had already been allowed to take the reins again. He beckoned His only Son and said: "Look, do you see, that little speck in the Westgaag: that's the boar-keeper's cart, there halfway between the Toll and the motorway — see, among the reeds by the water covered in all those waterlilies. They might be going slowly but they're making progress and that little boy is driving the horse."

I could see it in my mind's eye as clearly as if it were real and I heard the pig grunting and the boar-keeper chuckling, and the reed rasped in its throat. The man in the brown deerstalker was cycling further ahead and had not even looked round once. On and on we rode, without getting much further, and the boar-keeper kept on talking.

"Every evening Berend gets eight eggs, don't you, Berend?" He glanced back at the van. "And he downs them with liquorice — what a good fellow he is. The only thing is that he screws a bit clumsily; you'd think that by now he would have gained some experience, but not a bit of it. He makes heavy weather of it every time. It's as though he can't find the openings in the sows properly; perhaps they've all got it in a different spot. Now jumping up, he does that like the best of them, for all his weight, but his screwing still isn't as it should be. Well, I suppose it's much the same with people. Quite a job, it is, always on the go and sometimes there isn't a single sow on heat in the whole area and you're left high and dry. It's a funny thing, you know, but an animal or boar like that, it gets worn out from screwing. In my experience it's best to go easy, as a man; it wears you out."

He paused again and shook his head in concern.

"Berend's just about finished. I don't think he'll last much longer. I could have him castrated so he would make nice bacon but I don't think I could ever eat Berend. And I'll never sell him. You get attached to these animals, you know. I've become particularly attached to Berend. He's always good-natured, never gets ill, is fit, even though he's getting a little older, and his digestion gives no trouble — I've never had to get the vet — it's just, well, it's the screwing, you see, that's his weak point. Then again, it doesn't really matter. Better to screw badly than to screw like Klaas used to, the last one I had. He would whip it in as fast as we used to dip our hand in the collection plate if we needed a little extra money, but then what a racket he would make! All Maasland could hear how he was enjoying himself! Oh, Klaas, Klaas, you rooted yourself into the ground, tsk, tsk, tsk...well, I'll be damned, there's that fellow on the bike again. Pass me the reins, will you — yes, I know you're driving as though you've done it all your life, but all the same it's better for me to take them from you. Hey, you old weathercock, how much longer are you going to keep flapping up and down? I'm not pulling over for you again."

The man in the brown deerstalker passed us again, this time in the opposite direction, and he saw me and looked in astonishment before waving with a gleeful look on his face. We had come to the dual carriageway and had to wait for a long time since the boar-keeper would not cross until the road was completely clear. We stood there in sunlight and shade, the horse let its head droop and the occasional car sped by. Either to the right or to the left there was always a car to be seen in the distance and so we waited patiently for that one, quiet moment that simply would not come. It was as though we were dozing off, as though we were becoming fused with the Westgaag and the tall reeds along the road. The boar-keeper slumped back, his mouth fell open and he burst a bubble that had come to his lips. Very carefully he drew his cap down over his eyes and said: "Give the reins a tug if the road's really clear," and then he fell asleep, popping another bubble.

I looked up and down the road, determined not to set off until there was not a car in sight. We stood there and once again God looked down at us and was surprised that we were not going any further. Then the pig suddenly grunted, which gave me such a shock that I tugged at the reins and the cart lurched into motion while the boar-keeper slept on peacefully. We crossed the road and one car braked in front of us with an alarming noise, while a second car saw us coming and slowed down in time to let us pass. The driver of the first car got out, shouted something, and got in again. It all seemed as unreal as though I were asleep and dreaming on the box. But it was the boar-keeper who had blown a bubble which refused to pop. We rode along the road, which had become even narrower here, and I looked at the blank wall of a farm on which the sun was shining and the branches of an apple tree were casting a shadow. Further ahead the sun was reflected from the low-lying glass of melon-frames with such intensity that one was forced to avert one's eyes, and so I looked towards the polder that lay across the other side of the broad expanse of water. The two Maasland towers rose up on the horizon and I could see that the wind was dropping because in the distance the clouds hung motionlessly in the sky while those above me were drifting along much less quickly too. The horse trudged on until there came an irritable growl from the van. I looked round and saw that one of the pig's feet was stuck through one of the many gaps in the side of the cart. The growling failed to wake the boar-keeper up but did disturb his sleep; the bubbles disappeared and in their stead he mumbled something and at the same time the boar pushed open the door of the cart, which was only secured at the top with a chock, so that I could see the animal's snout. I nudged my neighbour.

"He's trying to get out," I cried.

"What, how?"

The cap was pushed back and the boar-keeper awoke. He looked about him in surprise, frowned and then laughed cheerfully.

"To think we nearly passed Stien! That's right, Berend, we've gone too far; we'll go back a bit. Well, I never! There he is inside the dark cart and unable to see a thing, and yet he knows exactly when we've passed Stien's sty, even though it's quite a few months since he served her. But then he's always had a weakness for Stien — now then, Berend, calm down, we are going back, but just a little further first because we can't turn here."

The pig nevertheless protested loudly when we drove on and pushed with all its might against the little door, so that the chock suddenly no longer held and the enormous head slipped out, while the grunting became even louder and angrier than before.

"Just hold on a moment, Berend. There's no need to force the door. You better watch it, or I'll take it off and then it will rain on your head and you'll be in a draught. Well, here we are. I'll just help you get down first — you've not got far to go now and we'll be going back. Come on, don't be so stubborn, let me help you — you could have broken a leg. Remember me to your father."

I dashed off, partly so as to complete the final section of the journey as quickly as possible, but also out of fear of that bellowing pig. Once I reached the bend, however, I slowed down. The wind had dropped completely and there were delicate spring scents in the air which made you feel dizzy. I walked on calmly, for there were houses everywhere; if the man in the dark-brown hat were to reappear I could walk into the nearest yard and call for help. Oddly enough, thanks to that man, I was less afraid of meeting God on a walk. I even felt I would never again be scared of God on foot, as though I knew that something like that simply did not exist and had never existed, except in the days of Enoch. God who walked along the road like an ordinary person. No, that didn't happen; I wasn't frightened of such a God any more. But I also knew that from now on I would always be frightened of men like the cyclist with the little brown hat and above all I knew that God could be present invisibly. Yes, it seemed for all the world as though I were already walking with God, because the wind had dropped and there was such an indescribably wonderful smell of life and spring in the air that I grew steadily smaller, a speck in the ever-expanding landscape. The Maassluis towers receded, the polder grew larger and larger and I became tinier, smaller than the smallest insect; I shrank, becoming almost invisible in a vast expanse. And that expanse itself, that steadily growing expanse, that was God. My heart pounded and my breath whistled and I ran along the water and the reeds and the wild yellow irises. I knew I had to hurry because it would not be much longer before I was taken away. And Enoch walked with God: and he was not; for God took him.

There was the house that belonged to Mrs Poot, the woman who owned the garden which my father rented. I ran through the yard past the house, saw my father standing in front of one of the greenhouses, and ran past the trolley, past the compost heap, past the greenhouses. My father saw me and looked more surprised than I had even seen him look before. I remained a speck in a limitless expanse until I clasped his legs and pressed my face against his corduroy trousers to dry my eyes on the material and to conceal from him that they were filled with tears. *Just in time,* I thought, *just in time;* and I knew that I had lost and was unworthy of God because, I realized acutely, I loved my father much, much more than God.

"Where's your mother?" he asked.

"At home," I said as loudly as possible into the black material of his trousers.

"Are you all by yourself then?"

"Yes, I came on foot."

"On foot, all that way? All by yourself?"

"Yes."

He suddenly lifted me up and I didn't know whether he was doing so from fury or from sheer happiness. But he proved to be neither furious nor happy and called out loudly: "Arie, Arie, just listen to this — my son's here, come all the way from Maassluis on foot by himself, it's unbelievable."

I heard the pride in his voice and I saw how our neighbour Mr Van der Hoeven looked at me in astonishment as I was held aloft, and yet I myself was not at all proud — simply relieved and unhappy because I knew myself to be unworthy in the eyes of God who had nearly taken me away and who now looked on angrily at how my father was lifting me up to Him, as if to show Him that I was his property and not His property.

"You're only just in time, you know," my father said. "I was just on my way to Ai Kip's because one of his hands is sick and he asked me if I would come and help him milk. If I had already gone you would have missed me altogether."

"Mr Kraan has been taken away," I said.

"Has he, now?" he said.

"And Uncle Job was cross with me because I was looking at the horses."

"The sod! There you are with two younger brothers — twins no less — and one of them, Huib, is a first-class fellow, but the other...."

He carried me high above his head through the garden. I told him about the coach, about Mrs Kraan, about the feather, and everything I said was directed not only towards him but also to Him who could see everything so well because I was being held aloft. He did not put me down until we had reached Mrs Poot's house, only to lift me up again a moment later to place me on the handlebars. And without delay we were under way in the now sunny, windless, shady Westgaag.

My father sang:

"O mother, please give me a ball,
You know it's the thing I adore,

The loveliest toy of them all

For playing with Jesus our Lord."

As he was singing the Maasland towers drew nearer and the polder
became smaller. The clouds were no longer drifting at such an unreal
height in the sky and I thought: *Now God can see me riding here and He
nearly took me away, here near the yellow flag.* What would He be
thinking now? At each word of the song my father was singing, the
distance between God and me became greater; each affectionate dig in
my back and each quick movement of his rough hand over my hair
reduced my fear of God. I thought: *If only He looks just as closely now as
he did when I was sitting next to the boar-handler, then He can't help
seeing that my father loves me too much to spare me.*

We rode into the yard at Ai Kip's farm. My father braked with his
clogs in the gravel, which made so much noise that the free-ranging
chickens sped off in all directions. My father lifted me off the
handlebars on to the ground. We walked to the enclosure behind the
stables. My father took a milking stool and greeted Ai Kip and his
oldest hand, Thijs Loosjes. He sat down by a red and white cow, which
surprised me since I had often heard him say: "Always shun the red
and dun," but perhaps there was no other cow available. I watched the
deft way in which he squeezed the teats. Both hands went up and
down in turn and a thin, white jet squirted regularly into the bucket. A
foaming mass was quickly built up consisting of thick bubbles that
would not burst. And above the foam, above the profusion of large
bubbles, there lay a fine, transparent mist, which was continually
separated by the thin white jet. I was allowed to help milk the second
cow, a black and white one. I had done it before but when I sat under a
cow by myself I was still afraid of the swishing tail and of the restless
movement with which a cow would toss back its head. I only dared
milk if my father was next to me, when it would assume something of
the nature of a miracle, for you didn't know why that precise motion
— running the fingertips down the teat with a certain force, with an
extra squeeze here and there and always maintaining a constant speed
— should make the milk squirt into the pail. There were thousands of
possible movements but only one of them was effective and you could
only learn that movement if you were not too afraid and had plenty of
patience. Next to us Thijs Loosjes was milking much more calmly
than my father.

"Still no plans for getting married?" my father asked him.

"No, why should I?"

"Well, you've been engaged for twenty years now."

"Much longer."

"All right, longer then. I simply don't understand it."

"Nobody's asking you to understand it."

"Haven't you got the least desire then to dive under the sheets with that woman of yours?"

"If I take her in she might want to sit at the same table as me."

"Well, what's wrong with that?"

"That's not for me. It's just right as it is. On Sundays I see her twice when we go to church together and that's quite enough; you can have the rest, thank you very much."

"In the past, when I was still working here and you were a foreman at the Leeuwenwoning, we had a bull who come what may refused to mount a cow. For a start you give it a couple of years because you expect such tantrums to blow over, but it didn't blow over and Ai Kip says to me: 'Pau, we'd better slaughter the beast. If we leave him alone we'll still be stuck with him in fifty years.' 'Well,' I say, 'it's not a good time to slaughter him — you've only got to hand it all over to the Huns. You'd be better off going to the vet and asking him to remove its driving licence; then you can fatten him up nicely until we're liberated.' 'No,' he says, 'we'll slaughter it on the sly.' Well, so we slaughter it on the sly in the cowshed and load it on to a cart, and I dug a hole to conceal the beast and we take it outside to the pit and I jump in to smooth out the bottom of the hole a bit and then I get this whacking great clout on the head. I thought at once: the Huns are here. But nothing was up — the bull's front leg had just slipped off the cart. We got many a good meal out of it; every now and then we dug it up and cut a piece off."

"What are you getting at?"

"Nothing, I'm just telling you because that bull was just like you. Do you really intend never taking it any further than an engagement?"

"Yes. I'll never get married."

"Well, never is a long time. I always used to think that I wouold never work for anyone again, and yet I'm thinking of moving on."

"What are you thinking of doing?"

"I've applied for a job with the council in parks and gardens. Or at the cemetery."

"At the cemetery?"

"Yes. In the past, when I used to walk past the cemetery at Boonersluis with my mother, I would say to her: 'I want to work there when I'm big.'"

"Has the council already taken you on?"

"I've got to go there later today. See the top brass. I think I'll knock off after this cow."

As we were standing by the gate and Ai Kip gave my father some money for the milking, the farmer suddenly said: "I've got a nice little plank, you know — I saw you coming with your son perched on the handlebars — and if you fixed it on top of them he could sit nice and comfortably. I don't need the plank any more."

"Well, let's see," said my father.

Ai Kip disappeared into a shed and returned with a round, wooden board that my father mounted onto the front of the bicycle. Then he lifted me up on to the plank and Ai Kip said, "What you need now are these two footrests I've got — stick them in here under the handlebars."

And the footrests were installed on the bicycle too and then we rode off. I sat on the plank more grandly than ever before. I was able to hold on to the handlebars much more easily and on my left and right I saw my father's enormous, hairy fists. I looked at his right hand, which was casually holding the handlebar grip. How innocent that hand looked! And yet I knew that my father liked nothing better than shaking people by the hand and I pictured to myself how, smiling pleasantly, he would shake hands for the first time with someone who did not know him and the person, his face distorted with pain, would quickly try to free his hand from my father's giant grasp and they would never succeed.

"What's up?" my father said to me. "You look as though you're suddenly in some sort of pain."

Even God, I thought, even God might wet His pants in pain if my father were to shake His hand, and the thought made me sigh, since it was so nice to think that even God might not be a match for my father. We cycled into the setting sun until we reached the Toll Gate. To begin with we could not see the sun when we riding on the dyke, because the road was screened off by the high hawthorn hedge. I could see myself running along behind that hedge again and I saw some smoke rising from the fire that had not been a burning bush and each time the bicycle jolted briefly over a concrete ridge in the road I resisted the impulse to look up at my father. No, he did not know what had happened there; he only knew about Mr Kraan and Uncle Job and the feather. And perhaps it would be better not to tell him about it; he

144

would be sure to say: "Why are you so afraid? There's no need to be afraid of anybody, just like I'm not afraid." I caught sight of the spot in the grass where I had lain to watch the man in the brown deerstalker, and I felt pleased at still being able to see where the grass had been flattened. That was where it had happened and now I was riding past with my father and could see the spot without being afraid.

We cycled on quietly and I counted how long we took between the concrete ridges. The hedge stopped at the Tin Shed and there was the sun low over the river — so red now that you could look at it without being blinded. An enormous ship was going out to sea on the river, its flags hanging limply, and a soundless train sped along the railway line that cut the polder between the dyke and the waterway in two. All I heard was the swish of the bicycle tyres and my father singing the words, "Daddy, dear, daddy dear, won't you come home," in his measured, deliberate and comforting voice. The sun rode along with us and for a moment I thought: would God be the sun? The Bible, after all, said that God was a blinding fire. If God was the sun He would see us riding there, my father and I, and He would see that there was no room for a third person but that it was as it should be. Enoch walked with God and I was riding with my father, level with Marie's house, and perhaps I was unworthy of God because I loved my father more than Him, but I did not care a bit, there, high on the dyke, on the front of the bicycle with hands on the handlebars and my feet firmly on the footrests, while my eyes glanced from the giant ball of fire across the river to the long, long shadows cast by my father and me speeding along the white concrete and seemingly going much faster than we were, although they never overtook us. It seemed as though we would ride there until the end of time, my father and I, and as though the sun would always remain poised just above the water. But our shadows suddenly disappeared when we entered the town and we could no longer see the sun because the low houses along the dyke were in the way.

We rode along Hoogstraat and my father said: "I'll leave you against the wall round the corner for a moment. You can get off or stay on, whatever you want; I'm going to have a word about the job I've applied for."

He placed his bicycle against the blind wall of the town hall, just by the steps leading down to the quayside behind the houses in Hoogstraat. I could see the sun again. It was so close to the water that there wasn't even any room for the little boat from Dirkzwager's shipping agency that was on its way out to collect the final messages from a big ship going out to sea. For a moment the boat obscured part of the sun, which I was able to see because both the railway bridge and the Kippen drawbridge were up. The boat disappeared and the sun touched the water and the harbour became a burning fire. I could not remember ever having seen that before, because I had never seen the railway bridge and the Kippen bridge up together at that brief instant in late afternoon when the sun and the water met. The sun lay there at the harbour entrance like an angry sentinel and I could not help thinking of the mysterious and disturbing biblical text: "So he drove out the man; and he placed at the east of the garden of Eden Cherubims, and a flaming sword which turned every way". All of a sudden I knew that the sun was there for me and that God had placed it there because I had turned away from Him that afternoon, just like Adam. I looked at the fiery water slapping between the quays and I thought in astonishment and guiltily, yet at the same time satisfied at the addition to my understanding: *So that is the water of life that proceeds out of the throne of God and of the Lamb.*

12
The monitor

As the seagull was greedily devouring the young bird, an unseen person switched on a light over a blackboard and a writing hand appeared in a round circle of light. The image of the white bird faded; the legs of the chick which were still sticking out of the beak faded too, and it seemed as though the seagull waited to swallow until the hand had inscribed its white words on the blackboard. The hand was unable to squeeze the whole message into the circle of light; the word telephone was partly obscured and was less clearly legible than: "Hart,...Leiden urgent," and it became dark again in the auditorium. The tribute to Niko Tinbergen continued with the showing of his film *Signals for Survival.* I hurried to the front, already quite certain of the reason for the interruption.

My brother-in-law was on the other end of line: "I've got bad news for you. Your father's in hospital. It's very serious. They want you to come at once."

I ran to the station, wondering the whole way whether it would not be quicker to take a tram or taxi. Once I was in the train I thought: *It's two months now since I tried telling him anything and all that time nothing happened.* But why hadn't I dared even drop a hint? Was it because I had resolved to wait for the first symptoms of the illness? But since the third of October there had been no sign of any illness. Or was the fact that my father had become steadily more bad-tempered in the past few months related to the tumour? At night, especially, so my mother had told me, he could become dreadfully angry. He would sit up straight in bed and shout: "I'll kill the lot of them, all those bastards who've tried to hold me down."

He would shout this out in his sleep and, waking himself up as a result, would sob at everything that had been inflicted on him. All the childhood humiliations he had still not come to terms with came to the surface, and he re-crossed the bridges of his youth. In his mind's eye he saw himself leaving home at thirteen and heard his father as he said goodbye: "At least we won't have to feed his carcase any more." When he had reached this stage in his nightly tale there generally followed a procession of Maasland gentleman farmers until finally the greatest monster of all appeared, the market-gardener Poot. I too was drawn into his rage because I was said "to have a good set of brains" but had abandoned the true faith and had married a woman who was not only too small and thin and wore glasses (which was particularly odd, for my mother too wore spectacles when my father had first met her), but who was an unbeliever.

During the train journey I thought of the birthday visit. A little over a week before he had visited me and had said, as he wished me many happy returns: "You couldn't give a damn that we've come to wish you happy birthday; we could just as well stay away. You'll be glad when we clear off."

The whole afternoon he had sat without moving in a chair, unusually silent for him and staring ahead irritably with those glittering green eyes which he could fasten on a dog so that it would first start to whine and then, its tail between its legs, run off at high speed. Only now and then did he open his mouth to say something: "If I always had to sit on chairs like you've got here my back would soon go. You're better off on one of the biers at the cemetery."

Then he had fallen silent again for a long time before observing abruptly and unexpectedly: "Why haven't you even got a photo of your mother and father here?"

"Why should I?"

"I suppose we're too humble, just like in that book by Bordewijk — that lawyer had tiny pictures of his parents on his desk and enormous ones of his parents-in-law."

"I haven't got any pictures of my parents-in-law either."

"No, because you are not prepared to admit that you would hang up big pictures of them and little ones of us."

"Whatever makes you think that?"

He had not replied but had just stared furiously in front of him, whistling softly but persistently at regular intervals. It was that whistling, which I knew so well from other times, that was particularly disturbing and whenever I had looked at him I had thought: *He's just like David Schearl's father in* Call it Sleep. *That's the sort of man he is, except you're usually unaware of it because he generally manages to convert his anger into his special brand of humour.*

I had in fact been relieved when he left in late afternoon; our house had been filled with a smell of boiled milk and pungent Van Nelle tobacco. Upon leaving he had said threateningly: "You're just as old now as I was when you were born."

After he had left I had opened windows and doors. That had enabled me to dispel the odours but my sense of resentment had remained. I had thought: *All those months I suffered grief on his account and vicariously came to terms with his death. But it has all been for nothing, he has not become ill. I sat in the dark next to my amplifier; I knocked an old man over and went off to the Binntal and raked leaves, all for his sake. But he had deceived me: there is no terrible illness. The only thing that happens is that he comes here and whistles.* Yes, I had been able to disperse the odours with fresh air but the whistling had hung in the room because it had already gone and so could not be driven out by opening a window.

I sat in the train, astonished at my resentment of the week before. Unbelievable! I had not been relieved at the fact that he had not become ill: no, it had been a case of resentment. If only he hadn't whistled, I thought, the notion of deception would never have occurred to me. But again I heard my tirade against God after my father had said grace on the third of October and I was no longer so sure.

I looked out over the polders in the rain and wondered that it should already be so dark so early in the afternoon. I looked at the barely moving horizon and thought again of Dickens's deceitful distance, realized suddenly that it was from *Dombey and Son,* and went on to think about Tom Pinch from *Martin Chuzzlewit.* It seemed as if a deeper, as yet unfathomed significance had all at once to be attributed to my father's comment that I was just like Tom Pinch. Pinch had not seen through Pecksniff, but was the only one to have esteemed and admired him while everyone else knew the architect to be a sanctimonious scoundrel. Was my attitude towards my father the same as Pinch's towards Pecksniff? Was my father a vulgar, uncultured man who took refuge in coarse jokes, and was I the only one not to see that?

I saw Hanneke standing in the rain on the platform at Leyden and I was relieved that I would not have to visit my father alone, because it seemed I would not be able to conceal my shame at the resentment I felt if I were to see him by myself. She knew which hospital he was in but did not know why he had been admitted so hurriedly. I too was surprised: could the tumour in the pancreas have erupted so suddenly and severely? All that time there had been nothing wrong: if anything he had seemed on the way back to the womb rather than to the grave, and now he was said to be in a critical condition. I found it very difficult to accept and could feel no satisfaction that it should be happening after all, even though it gave meaning again to the grief of the past few months.

We took a taxi southwards from the station to the hospital, and arrived at half-past five. I had assumed without thinking that I would be allowed to see my father straight away. But that was far from the case. An hour and a half before visiting hour, whatever did I expect! Come all the way from Amsterdam, as quickly as I could? Very good, because if his condition suddenly deteriorated we should all be close at hand. But at the moment there was no acute danger and so I could not see him. The doctor was attending to him and afterwards he would need to rest; it was even open to question whether we should be allowed to visit him at seven o'clock. But stay around, on no account go home again, because his condition could become critical again at any moment.

We sat on a bench in a dark corridor on the first floor, near the intensive care unit, and I thought: *The worst thing of all is that you should be admitted to and allowed to die in rooms with such names.*

My mother told me what had happened. At half-past eight, while Quaavers was with him in the shed, he had suddenly fallen flat on the floor, still fully conscious. He managed to get to his feet, sat down on a chair, and a doctor hastily summoned by Quaavers had at once diagnosed a heart attack and immediately sent him to the hospital. He had protested with all his characteristic fieriness, insisting that whatever happened he should be allowed to return home the next week to celebrate his birthday. To my mother, who had been hurriedly summoned, he had said: "I want to stay with you," and, by way of fond embrace, had pinched her so hard in the arm that the bruise was still visible in the half-light of the hall. Nevertheless he had been taken away in an ambulance with siren wailing. During the afternoon his heart had ceased beating but had been revived by massage.

When my mother had finished her account I did not hesitate for a moment. I told her about my visit to the doctor that fine spring evening, told her about the tumour in the pancreas, and it was as if I related it to comfort her and to tell her: "This heart attack is sparing him from a far more dreadful fate." In my thoughts I even used that idea to excuse my quite unnecessary candour. But at the same time I knew I was only telling her because I wanted to be rid of the secret — that I was unburdening myself because it was a relief to talk about it. It was more than relief; it was as though I could at last breathe freely and while I was talking it seemed as though none of it were true, and could not be true: my father would have fallen ill long ago if there really had been such a tumour.

Shortly after six the ward-sister let me see him briefly. He was lying quietly in bed and next to him each heartbeat was visible on a monitor as a green, moving line. Systole and diastole succeeded each other regularly, with only a small, erratic peak between them: a slight irregularity, nothing to get worked up about or to be afraid of.

"I was dead for two minutes this afternoon," he declared proudly. "They brought me back to life with heart massage. Is your mother still here?"

"Yes."

"There's no need for her to hang about. There's nothing wrong."

"She's allowed to visit you in three-quarters of an hour, at seven o'clock — she'll stay till then."

"Seven o'clock? Impossible, it's around three now."

"No, it's already gone six."

"Impossible. Do you know they brought me in an ambulance this morning with the siren blaring? The first time, you know! You've never been in one of those things, have you? Another first for me!"

"No, I've never been taken by ambulance."

"You can't hear the siren at all."

"Perhaps because you...."

"Not a bit of it. I was fully conscious, and yet I didn't hear a thing. Well, and after that I was brought here and they've been fiddling with me all day and now it's three o'clock."

The sister in the cubicle waved to me that I should go. I got up.

"I'll be back home next week to celebrate my birthday," he said. "I'll be older than my brother Maarten then."

"You are now."

"Yes, but then you can really tell. Then I'll be fifty-eight while he only lived to fifty-seven."

"I'm off. You'll have visitors again at seven."

"Your mother?"

"Yes."

"Fine. Won't you be coming?"

"I should think so."

But I was not allowed to visit him at seven; only my mother was allowed to see him because he had to stay as quiet as possible. His was the most serious case in the ward and he was closest to the observation cubicle with the six monitors registering six heartbeats of six people who would already have long been dead if such technology had been less advanced.

When my mother returned shortly before the end of visiting hour she was crying. "Hanneke's allowed to visit him for a minute," she said. "He prayed with me, taking both my hands like this and folding them around his own folded hands, and then he prayed out loud to be allowed to get better. 'I so much want to stay alive a little longer, for my wife and children', he said to the Lord, 'but not my will but thy will be done.' "

As she was telling me it seemed all at once as though the whistling of the week before was no longer of any account and as though my resentment disappeared. That was *my father; that was* my father, the man who defied all and everyone, who had prayed without embarrassment in a hospital ward, so loudly that others could hear him.

Hanneke rejoined us and said: "He asked me if I would forgive him for having always been so unpleasant to me. 'It's all right, don't worry,' I told him."

The ward-sister appeared: "One of his family is allowed to stay the night, the others will have to go home." My brother wanted to stay and I wanted to stay. I stayed because I was the eldest. The others left. I sat there in a tiny waiting-room, with nothing to read except the usual faded magazines. The traffic swished past outside on the motorway and that disturbed me. It was not quiet in the building; doors kept banging and I could hear footsteps drawing closer and each time I would imagine that the footsteps were on their way to the little waiting-room. I sat down on the bed and mumbled all the poems by Bloem I knew. In all I knew perhaps thirty, and it was surprising how quickly I had recited them all. But I began all over again and the poems almost became adjurations; it was as though they had been specially written for those circumstances. I also muttered some other poems, but they had nowhere near the force of Bloem's — not even Emily Dickinson's poems. From time to time a speeding car swished past outside. On one occasion the approaching footsteps in the corridor were indeed bound for my waiting-room.

"You can see your father if you want. He's quiet now, but make sure you don't stay long — just say good night."

I walked along the corridor. He was very close, just two doors along. I opened the door. He was lying quietly on the bed. He appeared to be asleep. Even the unevenness between the systole and diastole had disappeared; his heart was beating more peacefully than mine. I went up to the bed and tapped his hand very gently with one finger. He instantly opened his eyes.

"Are you still here?" he asked.

"Yes."

"Are you staying?"

"Yes."

"Can you sleep here?"

"Yes, in a little waiting-room two doors along."

"Your mother gone home?"

"Yes."

"Just as well, she badly needs some rest."

"I've come to say good night."

"Good. I still don't believe for a minute that I'm going to die."

"No, you look perfectly all right again. Good night."

I wanted to leave again, for she had said: "Just say good night." Moreover I wanted to avoid tiring him in any way. What he needed now was rest — the first night, that was what mattered and what he had to get through.

"Don't go just yet," he said.

"No, I'm off. You need as much rest as possible. 'Bye, sleep well."

"Come on, don't go just yet."

But I walked off and waved to him, and the girl in the observation cubicle smiled at me. He closed his eyes and seemed to fall asleep instantly, which may well have been so, for he was able to drop off from one moment to the next, and I thought that could even prove his salvation, that he sleeps so soundly.

As I walked back to my room I was convinced that next morning I would find him as lively as a cricket and that would mean he had pulled through, for I knew the first twenty-four hours were critical in the case of a heart attack. And although it was still early I simply went to bed: what else was there to do? I rather regretted having allowed myself to be intimidated by the nurse and that I had not stayed longer. But it was better like that, for he needed to lie quietly and to sleep; that

153

way he should get through the night. I lay in bed but could not sleep. Once again I recited Bloem's thirty poems, again carefully avoiding "In Memoriam", however much I admired it, because "In Memoriam" did not as yet arise, and I did not want to think about it. At the same time I thought: *If it really is true that he's got a head of the pancreas carcinoma it would be better for him to die of a heart attack now than to remain alive and die a terrible death later on.* But it was a rather bleak and shadowy thought, as though one had to choose between two dreadful alternatives, and if he were to get through this night he would at least stay alive for some time — admittedly with a tumour in the pancreas, but the tumour appeared to be dormant, or perhaps a miracle had occurred. Miracles did, after all, happen very occasionally in the case of cancer patients for whom there had been thought to be no hope.

Meanwhile the cars continued to hum past. They kept me from a sleep which would not have come anyway. I kept on muttering Bloem's thirty peoms and regretted that I did not know more. I resolved to learn all his other poems by heart as well, particularly if my father should live, since I might well be in need of them again. I thought also of the other poems I ought to learn by heart, and the first that came to mind was naturally "Night" by Obe Postma. But didn't I already know it by heart? I tried to recite it. But while I recalled it perfectly I did not know how all the Frisian words were meant to be pronounced and so I got up from the bed and wrote it out, on the back of the Tinbergen tribute programme.

I looked at the poem as though it were a painting and knew that it meant so much to me because it was as if it were about my father and my mother and myself when I had still been with them. Then, as in the poem, the night used to go round the house and we had listened, each with our own dream, and everything that had long since sunk had sailed again on the stream of life. Had my mother waited for something, like the second stanza said? Certainly it had been a matter of bloom; I saw her before me, still so young, and she had been *"maitids-blank"*. How ever should one translate that? With the beauty of spring? Pale as May time? And, as the wind swept through the wintry yard, my father had set out on a storm-tossed path. Stormy weather it had been, too, when I had walked to meet him, the tree-tops creaking. And true it was too that I, the child, had dreamed of a coloured picture, a picture in which there had not been a king or fairy, but in which there had been a little boat. It was a picture of the boat

154

that Jesus had protected, and which my father had stuck on to hardboard and sawn into a jigsaw. But why did those last two lines keep bringing tears to my eyes?

And venturing in its little boat
Sets out for unknown seas.

I tried to lull myself to sleep with those last two lines. But every time the "caught in separate dreams" would startle me just as I was dropping off. What was my father's dream? Beating Uncle Klaas at billiards and having a mixed farm with cows and some arable land? Why did it bother me that that was so far removed from my own dreams? What for that matter was my own dream? I did not even know, but it was of no account; all that mattered was that it was a totally different dream from my father's. If our dreams had only been more closely attuned I would have managed to say something after the visit to the GP, I persuaded myself. Or had I cowardly avoided a confession, or the beginnings of one? Or had I in fact wanted to talk about it in order to be rid of the secret, although it was better to remain silent, and did I feel guilty as a result? I had cycled to him in the spring and had raked leaves with him in autumn, but all the same I had drawn back from alluding to something I simply did not know whether to talk about or not. And now, before he had been able to say anything, I had slipped off. "Come on, don't go just yet." Why hadn't I stayed? For fear of the sister? For fear of what he might say? "If he should die tonight," I said aloud, "how can I ever accept the fact that I went away when he asked me to stay?" For that reason alone it seemed out of the question that he would die that night. Even when I walked to meet him as a small child, I thought, I kept the most important thing from him and did not tell him what had happened on the dyke. It suddenly seemed as if that had been the start of so much more that had been concealed and as if this had culminated in the suppression of the information I had received from the doctor. Perhaps, despite the difference in our dreams, there had after all existed a surprisingly great harmony between us, because I had concealed so much. I had remained silent because I had loved him, and because he was so hard to approach and knew how to shelter behind his jokes and stories. And then there was the additional difficulty of his profession: I could not talk with him about death because he was lord and master of the subject and dealt with it daily.

Once again I saw the line on the monitor before me. *He's sure to pull*

155

through, I thought, *and then I'll still have loads of time to disagree with him instead of listening to his jokes and lively stories. He will recover and there is no question of a carcinoma of the head of the pancreas, that's simply not possible, in that case he would have been dead long ago. Yes, he'll recover and then I'll show him I'm not a Tom Pinch, then I'll take up cudgels with him, and he with me: then there'll be more points of friction than just those about Hitler and* Karakter, *then we'll really come to grips with each other and that might be at the expense of the harmony between us, that sense of mutual confidence, of us against the rest of the world, but we'll have a better idea of what we mean to each other.*

I lay waiting for footsteps and dozed. Was I dreaming or was I just resurrecting memories? My father and I were looking at a beautiful bouquet of white lilies that had been delivered by a heavily-built man who informed us that it was to be placed on the grave of the crew of the *Volharding.* Immediately afterwards the man left. My father, singing about the girl who had been given a ball and had fallen in the canal and drowned, had found a pewter vase and placed it on the plot under the chestnut trees.

"Such a fine bunch," my father said, "and the fellow doesn't even wait to see where it's put but leaves straight away. If I had simply thrown them away he couldn't have cared less."

It was autumn. It had been glorious weather all day and a little cloud of small, mourning mosquitoes were suspended over the gravestone of the captain of the *Volharding.* The odd cricket was still chirping in the little hedges around the plots in front of the gravestones and a querulous wind rustled among the birches. From near the rhododendron bush came the soft trill of a robin redbreast, while swallows massing to migrate twittered in the sky.

My father looked up at the sky and said: "We might be in for a spot of ground frost."

"Yes, there's a real nip in the air," I said.

"Might be better to stick those lilies in the shed for the night."

"Yes, otherwise they might be dead tomorrow."

"Or should we take them home for the night? The air's cold enough for them to get ruined even in the shed."

"You're right — there's no cloud cover and we could get quite a frost."

"You can say that again," he said, wiping the sweat from his brow.

My father took the lilies out of the pewter vase and walked to the exit, and I followed him. It was warm late-summer weather and I heard my father's footsteps on the gravel because he was wearing clumping clogs. Then a door banged, there were more footsteps, and someone knocked at the door of my room.

"Yes," I called.

An unfamiliar nurse opened the door.

"Your father's not too well after all. You'd better go to him. He's fighting for his life."

I sprang out of bed. She gave me a towel and soap.

"You can freshen up next door and then it might be best if you gave your mother a ring."

I washed and got dressed. It was just before five, I saw from my watch. I rang my mother. She answered the phone straight away as if she had been waiting beside it all night.

"I've been lying on the floor in the sitting-room," she said.

"You'd better come straight away," I said. "Things aren't too good after all."

I walked along the corridor to the window. I wanted to go to my father but felt it would be out of place for me to go alone. I should wait for my mother. And so I gazed at the approach road leading to the motorway.

But the unfamiliar sister came up to me and said urgently: "You'd better go to your father."

I went to the room where he was being nursed. When I opened the door he looked up for a moment, mumbled something that might have been my name, and tried to pull the intravenous tube from his arm. The sister, who sitting next to him and holding his left arm, stopped him. He tried to throw off the sheets and to swing his legs out of bed and the sister said to him half-beseechingly and half-sternly: "Just keep quiet, lie down, lie down."

I grasped his right hand and he struggled to free it. He still had a lot of strength, despite the strange flickering green line on the monitor which was moving wildly across the screen and sometimes even failed to rise. He muttered incessantly but I could not understand what he was saying, except that I sometimes thought I caught the word "away". The muttering was strangely alarming. But even stranger was the expression in his eyes. It was as though he saw nothing and there was a film before his eyes. From time to time we had to push him gently — or not so gently — but firmly back into bed and he fought and struggled to get free, not from us, but from something he wanted to run away from and sometimes he said so too, although the word "away" was then barely intelligible.

Time and again he sank back in the pillows and then sat up again. I was struck by how peaceful it was in the room otherwise; I could see the five other monitor screens in the observation cubicle. My father's line was not the only irregular one but at least a systole and diastole were visible in all the others. But no longer in my father's. Sometimes he moved is arm as though trying to swim against a current; sometimes he would after all suddenly get both his legs on the edge of the bed, always on the side where the sister was sitting, who would then push them back and speak to him as one speaks to a naughty child. Once again he threw off the sheets, tugged at the intravenous tube, and wrestled with an invisible oppenent who was pushing him back under the sheets. Once more he sat upright and desperately kicked away the sheets which the sister had already replaced. Then he suddenly slid to one side, towards me, fell back against the edge of the pillows and let out two small puffs, just as I had so often seen him do when he tried to blow smoke-rings. On the monitor the line suddenly became flat and still and contracted into a green, increasingly bright point that finally drifted towards the middle of the screen and whistled softly but with increasing urgency for attention.

The sister hurriedly switched the machine off and said: "It's all over."

She went away. I remained sitting. He was still lying on the edge of the pillows, his eyes half-open and his head a little to one side, and his hands still clenched. I shifted him into the middle of the bed and then two sisters appeared who detached all sorts of tubes and wheeled him away from under my very hands. I went out into the corridor to the window that looked out onto the access road and marvelled that my father had died so soon after I had come in. I looked at the dim street lights on the access road. At that moment a car turned the corner and its headlights cast a dull light on the wet asphalt. To my own amazement I heard myself say in a matter-of-fact voice: "Just too late."

My mother got out first, followed by my brother-in-law. They went in by a side-entrance and I went down the stairs to meet them.

"He's gone," I said to my mother.

We ascended the stairs in silence, walked in silence to the room where the bed had been wheeled. My brother-in-law opened the door and we saw two sisters at his bed, one of whom impatiently motioned: "Shut the door."

"Oh, they're laying him out," my mother sighed.

A few minutes later we were allowed to go to him. The two sisters shut the door behind us and we stood around the bed and he looked quite different from how he had looked immediately after those last two gasps. Then it had been as if he had struggled and lost with dignity; now he was so unrigged, so utterly dead, that I reproached myself bitterly for having left him alone for those few minutes. We just stood there, looking at him; I looked at his mouth that had fallen in so much during the short interval. Then we walked slowly along the corridor to the stairs and spoke briefly with the sister who had woken me, who expressed her sympathy and asked if we agreed to a post-mortem. I nodded. We descended the stairs and walked along the corridor leading to the night-entrance. It was an astonishingly long corridor and I felt as though we were taking hours, and, moreover, halfway we met a group of three people in the dimly lit gloom going in the opposite direction. They were laughing happily. A girl sitting in a wheelchair and holding her protuberant stomach with both hands laughed especially gaily. She was being pushed along by a boy who was equally happy and the nurse tripping along beside the wheelchair smiled encouragingly at the girl and talked continuously to her. They were past us in a flash: my mother, it turned out later, had not even seen them.

"Night" by Obe Postma

The night goes round the silent house;
They listen, caught in separate dreams.
'Tis roaming time: what long since sank
Sails once more on the living stream.

What might the woman be waiting for?
A miracle! That she again
Might bloom, and pale as spring unfold?
O night! O dancing lights of thought!

The wind sweeps through the wintry yard;
The man goes down the storm-tossed path;
Astray! O wild, unbridled life!
O complex fount of strange journeys.
The child dreams of its coloured print,
The magic world of kings and feys,
And venturing in its little boat
Sets out for unknown seas.